EDWARD RED

By A. J. Butcher

The Spy High Series
1. The Frankenstein Factory
2. The Chaos Connection
3. The Serpent Scenario
4. The Paranoia Plot
5. The Soul Stealer
6. The Annihilation Agenda

The Spy High Adventures
Edward Red
Angel Blue
Benjamin White
Calista Green
Jake Black
Agent Orange

EDWARD RED

a Spy High novel

A. J. Butcher

www.atombooks.co.uk

A paperback original from *Atom* Books

First published in Great Britain by Atom 2004

Copyright © 2004 by Atom Books

Based on concepts devised by Ben Sharpe
Story by A. J. Butcher

A CIP catalogue record for this book is available from the British Library.

ISBN 1 90423 334 1

Typeset in Cochin by M Rules
Printed and bound in Great Britain
by Bookmarque Ltd, Croydon

Atom
An imprint of
Time Warner Book Group UK
Brettenham House
Lancaster Place
London WC2E 7EN

www.twbg.co.uk

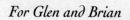

For Glen and Brian

PROLOGUE

It had been nicknamed Tinseltown for over a hundred years, but tonight Hollywood did more than sparkle. It shone. In the immediate vicinity of the Schwarzenegger Memorial Theatre its shimmering glory lit up the sky like an angelic host, and the hundreds of people braving broken ribs to cram closer to the stars cheered and whooped their approval.

It was the night of the Academy Awards Presentation 2064.

Security men with faces of stone and bodies of steel lined the route the limousines took, an impassable human barrier between the idolising and the idolised. There was a fusillade of camera flashes each time one of the sleek dark vehicles purred to a halt and disgorged the latest in a long line of visions of elegance and style. They waved to their fans, they smiled dentally recalibrated smiles, like gods acknowledging their worshippers. Lara Latimer. Brad Fox. Kelly O'Shaughnessy. Tiger Lee Trent. Names to set the heart racing and the imagination dreaming. Processing towards the theatre like priests.

Laughing among themselves, congratulating each other for being who they were. And appearing surprisingly contented for people in their final moments of life.

Inside the theatre, anticipation was building to a crescendo like water being brought to the boil. The ceremony was about to begin. Those fortunate enough to be present confined their ten thousand dollar suits and their drapes of diamonds to their allocated seats, determined not to move again until the Oscars were awarded and the parties ready to begin. Eager eyes settled on the stage.

So very few people actually noticed a handful of the younger members of the audience seeming to grow prematurely restless, glancing about, almost making eye contact one with another, as if they were part of a group though seated in different sections of the auditorium. Then they were getting to their feet. Moving towards the exits, and with an obvious sense of urgency, as if they were keen to get somewhere. Or to leave somewhere else behind them.

Two of the group found themselves striding side by side, both young men of about seventeen. The first, the one with the shaven head and the permanent sneer, like a scar that wouldn't heal, was flexing his fingers as if impatient to press a button. His red-haired companion carried his fists clenched.

'Did you do it?' hissed Shaven Head. 'Is it primed?'

'Of course,' Red Hair returned, assuming the answer sufficient for both questions.

'Good.'

The lights dimmed in the auditorium for the commencement of the ceremony, but it seemed unlikely that Shaven Head was referring to the awards.

Outside, the crowd was still encircling the theatre, ebbing and flowing, breaking against it like surf. The two young men had to physically force their way through.

'Hey, didn't you guys just, like, come out of the theatre?' asked a wide-eyed teenage girl. 'You're not *famous*, are you?'

'Not yet,' said Shaven Head.

And when they'd pushed and shoved a path to the rear of the crowd, when they could breathe easily again and they were beyond the ring of lights, fringed by darkness, they stopped and consulted their watches, the number displays on which had nothing to do with the time.

'We did good,' savoured Shaven Head. 'Plenty of leeway. We could be back at base before it blows. Not that I'd miss it for anything.'

Shaven Head twisted his watch face ninety degrees. Suddenly it bore only a single numeral, zero, and that was flashing.

The Schwarzenegger Memorial Theatre exploded.

Its walls shook but withstood the blast. Its windows and doorways did not. Fire spouted from them all, instantly incinerating anyone close by. Security men lit up like torches. The front ranks of the crowd crisped where they stood as white flame gushed over them. Cries of pleasure became screams of pain. The survivors turned to flee, the weak tripping, falling, trampled unwittingly by those behind them with no thought in their terrified minds but escape.

The hysterical mass of humanity surged irresistibly towards the onlooking boys. Neither of them seemed unduly concerned.

Because at that moment, every screaming voice was

silenced and every pounding limb was stilled. The scene froze, became tableau and timeless.

'He's stopped it already.' Shaven Head seemed disappointed.

'I know. Downer,' complained Red Hair. 'I'd have liked to have seen a few more crushed to death, even if they are only animates. And let's get a few more women and children in there next time as well.'

Shaven Head regarded his companion with narrow-eyed suspicion. 'You trying to be funny, Neilson?'

'Funny?' Red Hair looked surprised. 'What's funny about our noble struggle against the decadent democracies?'

'You know, Neilson,' Shaven Head thrust his sneering face forward, 'there's something about you I don't like.'

'If it's personal hygiene, it's not my fault the showers in this place only seem to work on a part-time basis.'

'Yeah, you're a funny guy, Eddie, a real funny guy. But between you and me, I don't know why Alazi let you join the Anarchy Academy in the first place. I don't think you understand the point of being a student here. 'Cause there are two kinds of people in the world, Eddie, the weak and the strong. The rest of us are training here 'cause we want to side with the strong. You, though, I've got a feeling you still get the hots for the weak. Which means I'm gonna be watching you in future. And I mean *close*.'

'Really?' The boy called Eddie Neilson didn't retreat from Shaven Head one inch. 'Frankie, I didn't know you cared.'

'Garvey. Neilson. Jackal Team. Gather round.'

While Eddie and Frankie Garvey had been squaring up to each other, the Hollywood sky had been retracted, rolled back like a blind, to reveal the truth of their location. They were in the jungles of Colombia, overlooked only by mountains, on a site that had years ago been cleared and on which a school had then been built, a special kind of school, the kind which required total secrecy to function properly, and where there was only one subject on the curriculum: terrorism. Now the hunched figure of the headmaster of the Anarchy Academy, Haroun Alazi, the man responsible for the Mount Rushmore outrage, approached. He walked with a limp, legacy of an American bullet and a narrow escape in his youth.

'Good work, Jackal Team. Fine work.'

Frankie Garvey contemptuously turned his back on Neilson, the better to hear his headmaster's praise. Eddie found time to glance again at the gutted replica of the Schwarzenegger Memorial Theatre, the trampled animates with their mouths stretched wide in perpetual agony. He considered such an atrocity happening for real. It was as well that Shaven Head couldn't see his face then.

'You all knew your tasks and you executed them faultlessly,' Alazi was continuing. 'Each of you is a credit to this Academy and will make heroic examples for the next generation of international freedom fighters. This will be the Anarchy Academy's highest profile operation yet, the beginnings of a new strategy. Why should we concern ourselves with political targets and the assassination of national leaders? Most of the ignorant, materialistic masses these days do not even know who their so-called leaders *are*. But their movie stars, their pin-up people, ah, now that is a different matter. A strike at their heroes is a strike at their hearts. So, even though today's rehearsal has been successful, we will practise again, and again. We will practise until our actual performance *cannot* go wrong.'

'Don't worry, sir,' assured Frankie Garvey. 'Nothing'll go wrong. Trust us.'

'Ah, Garvey,' admonished the headmaster, wagging the stump of his left hand's index finger, another victim of western imperialist aggression, 'you forget the Academy's cardinal rule: trust nobody.'

Eddie lay in his bed and stared at the ceiling, willing time to accelerate. If it didn't endanger the mission to secure his objective earlier than planned, he'd be up and about it right now. The sooner he could drop the pretence the better. He didn't know how he'd managed to remain in the role of Eddie Neilson, trainee terrorist and wannabe mass-murderer *this* long. He certainly couldn't keep it going indefinitely. Didn't have the stomach for it. That psychopath Frankie Garvey was already starting to smell a rat and some of the others mightn't be far behind. In this place the odour of vermin was one with which everyone was familiar.

Only minutes left, though. Patience. Two years of training at the Deveraux College had taught him the value of many things, waiting for the right moment being one of them. Soon he'd be able to revert to Eddie Nelligan, Spy High graduate and secret agent extraordinaire, the spy with a smile. Ben Stanton, another undercover operative, had signed him 0200 hours across the crowded and hopefully oblivious mess hall. They'd stayed incognito for as long as had been necessary to discover the academy's latest plan. Now they were going to do their bit to put Alazi and his staff of assorted lunatics out of business for good.

Eddie slipped out of bed and into the grey overalls that constituted uniform at the Anarchy Academy. His gaze flashed from one bed to the next, but his dormitory comrades seemed sound asleep, no doubt dreaming sweet dreams of anthrax alerts or explosions in public places. It evidently wasn't only those clear of conscience who slept well.

Eddie eased out of the dormitory and into the corridor. He moved swiftly along it. Everything had to be synchronised. He had to have Alazi before the other Spy High agents infiltrated computer control, immobilised the academy's automatic defences and signalled the authorities. They didn't want the headmaster performing another of his notorious narrow escapes and relocating the school elsewhere. Eddie had already promised himself: no more lessons in Innocent Bystanders. This sick parody of education was going to end.

There were guards outside Alazi's study, two of them. Good. So the terrorist leader hadn't chosen tonight to break his habit of working through until three. They were both armed. Even better. Eddie wasn't, and he was sure he could persuade them into a loan.

'Where do you think you're going?' Twin shock blasters, standard issue, were levelled at Eddie's chest.

'Mr Alazi's sent for me.' Eddie was innocence personified. 'Neilson. Jackal Team. It's to discuss my recent grades. Didn't he tell you?'

'No, he didn't,' said one of the guards. 'Wait here while I check.' He turned away.

This was also excellent. It meant that, when Eddie suddenly doubled up and groaned as if an explosive implant had gone off in his chest, the guard had a perfect view, and did what anyone of limited training and intelligence *would* do, utter 'What?' and take an incautious step forward. Directly into collision with Eddie's fist as, from being coiled and tensed, he sprang open again. The second guard had half-turned to the door, shock blaster requiring redirection if it was going to threaten Eddie. He didn't let it happen. Guards' skulls were legendarily thick, but not as thick as corridor walls. Or as hard.

'Yeah,' said Eddie, as he stood over the fallen bodies of the guards, 'my grades are so bad he thinks I shouldn't be here. And you know what, guys? He's right. But don't worry. I hear you can get fine headache medication in the penal satellites these days.'

Eddie switched the guards' shock blasters to stun. Spy High students didn't stoop to the same level as their enemies. The difference between stun and kill settings, a single click.

He'd probably receive an academy demerit for not knocking on his headmaster's door before entering. But he'd learn to live with it.

Haroun Alazi was hunched over his desk leafing through papers. He wasn't expecting to be disturbed, not least by a member of the student body wielding matching shock blasters. 'Neilson?'

'Not any more, sir.' Eddie fired at the headmaster's remaining fingers as they jabbed for the smart-desk's alarm. Alazi cried out as his arm stiffened uselessly. The alarm was untouched. 'And I'd sooner you didn't do that. There'll be an alarm soon enough.'

'What are you talking about?' Alazi pushed his chair back from the desk.

'When someone spots the incoming US Special Forces. Which, if my team-mates have done their jobs as impressively skilfully as I have, headmaster, sir, should be about now.'

The jarring wail of klaxons echoed through the academy.

'Am I a genius or what?'

'You're dead, boy, that's what you are!' Alazi's good hand reached to his boot. Then there was the eager gleam of a knife, flung upwards, slicing the air in two.

Eddie saw, and in the field to see and to react had to be the same thing. Otherwise a secret agenting career would be tragically and bloodily brief. He swivelled to the left, the blade skimming past his right side, and simultaneously fired with the blaster in his left hand. Alazi was struck full on the chest. With a gurgle he slumped back on his chair, chin drooping. Another enemy who'd wake in rather reduced circumstances. Eddie grinned.

Frankie Garvey slammed into him from behind, sending one shock blaster spilling to the floor. Eddie tried to get a shot in with the other. A well-aimed karate blow paralysed his arm. The second weapon dropped too.

'I told you I'd be watching you, Neilson.' The hatred was nearly as violent as the attack. Eddie was on the defensive, trapped against the desk. 'I told you I didn't like you. Now I know why.' In a flurry of fury. 'You're an establishment stoolie. You're an agent of the decadent imperialists. You're a *traitor*.'

'Hey, but Frankie,' Eddie retaliated, blocking the assault as best he could, 'at least I get dates.'

'You won't,' snorted Garvey. 'Not the way I'm gonna leave you.'

A hammer blow in the stomach. This time Eddie doubled up in pain for real, exposing his neck. Garvey's hand descended like a guillotine. And then Eddie thought his eyes must have burst because he could see only scarlet, like the world had turned to blood. His brain was on fire. His knees had snapped. Somehow, he'd fallen to them. And Frankie Garvey had hold of his hair, hold of his shock blaster.

'You're pathetic, Neilson, you know that?' Garvey was ranting instead of ending it. 'You think you're clever, don't you, think you're good? But you're not. You're nothing. I'm better than you. I'm stronger. I'm faster. And you know what?' Garvey switching the blaster back to kill. 'I'm gonna prove it.'

In the haze of Eddie's vision, the barrel of the blaster blurred. Garvey's finger tightened on the trigger.

But the shockblast came from the corridor. Accompanied by a voice. Ben's? Garvey had released his grip, forced to divert his fire. But Eddie didn't have the strength to take advantage of this unexpected turn of events. He slumped to the floor, looking on dazedly as Garvey and Ben exchanged one further blast each before the trainee terrorist bolted from the study and Eddie's team-mate, rather than taking off in pursuit, dropped to a crouch by his side and helped him sit up.

'You okay, Ed?'

'The 'ead's not so bad. It's the rest of me I'm worried about.' A firm believer in the power of humour to relieve stress, was Agent Nelligan. 'Ben, you can't let Garvey escape.'

'He won't get far. You sure you're all right?'

'I'll be fine. Not so much saved by the bell as saved by the Ben, huh?' Eddie winced, not entirely as a result of physical pain. 'I guess I'm the only one who needed the nick-of-time routine, though, yeah?'

'You did your job,' said Ben, glancing towards the unconscious headmaster. 'You took out Alazi. What more do you want?'

What about blond hair, blue eyes, a square jaw and a couple of extra inches in height, like you, Eddie thought.

Ben helped him stand. 'Come on, let's help the others with the round-up.'

The jungle night outside was thick with choppers like metal mosquitoes. Their spotlights glared pitilessly down on the Anarchy Academy like the eyes of multiple suns. Bond Team's disabling of the school's defences, coupled with the hour of the attack, had made the Special Forces' job easier and helped keep casualties to a minimum. It was all over bar the shouting – in a range of languages.

Eddie picked out the rest of the Spy High team, brandishing their weapons, caught in the white frame of the spots. Lori. Jake. Cally. Bex. 'Ladies and gentlemen,' he said, 'I give you the class of 2064. Appearing together for the final time.'

'Final time?' Ben questioned. 'Yeah, I guess you're right, Ed. When we get back we get allocated our graduate regions.'

'What you might call a new beginning.' Eddie didn't seem outrageously keen.

'I think so. Still – ' Ben surveyed the scene, Alazi's

next generation of international terrorists marching mind-calmed into custody – 'at least we're going out on a high. Mission accomplished.'

'Mission accomplished,' said Eddie.

But when the final list of prisoners was compiled, it seemed that one student was still unaccounted for. Frankie Garvey.

It was going to be like leaving home. Not so much the good parts about leaving home, either, the staying up late and never having to tidy your room parts, but the bad stuff, the missing people, the lack of familiarity, the idea of something lost that could never be regained. But there was no alternative. Once graduated, Spy High operatives became part of a worldwide network of secret agents – young, brilliant, at the cutting edge of the espionage business. A sure-fire way of having to fight the girls off with a stasis rifle, it had occurred to Eddie, before it had also occurred to him that his true line of work could never be revealed to anyone who wasn't already aware of Spy High's existence, not even in the noble cause of trying to pull. Each graduate would be given a cover story and a cover identity along with their placement.

As for his fellow graduates, the teamers he'd risked his life with and for over the past two years – it was time to say goodbye.

Eddie trooped dutifully along with the others to Mr Deveraux's rooms.

'Remember when we thought Jonathan Deveraux was actually human?' said Ben, exemplifying the generally nostalgic mood.

'I remember when he actually *was*,' said Bex. As Jonathan Deveraux's only child, that was not perhaps surprising.

'And he turned out to be a computer program.' Ben shook his head reflectively.

'You learn something every day,' remarked Eddie. He hoped that what he was about to learn concerning his graduate placement was going to be to his liking.

The founder's rooms preserved a perfectly controlled environment, the air-conditioning adapting automatically on the entry of six new heat sources in order to maintain the optimum temperature for the delicate instruments and circuitry that were housed here, the cyber-synapses of Jonathan Deveraux's brain. The late Mr Deveraux observed his students with two types of eyes. Firstly, the sensors in every panel of the mosaic floor monitored their movements, their vital signs, every nuance of their physical presence. Then, more conventionally, a pixellated portrait of the man who'd once been limited to flesh and blood – grey-haired, austere, almost regal – stared down at the visitors unblinkingly from the circle of screens that angled inwards from the ceiling.

'Bond Team,' he said. 'Welcome.' In a voice that was human and yet not human, that spoke words but conveyed no feeling.

Since they'd learned the truth about Jonathan Deveraux, Eddie had done a lot of thinking about how it must have been for Bex. How it must have felt to discover that the father she believed to be dead, whom she'd coffined away in her mind, was in reality still alive – or at least, his personality was, surviving as software and saving the world from the forces of darkness and terror.

He'd have liked to help her come to terms with it, had in fact offered his services in that general direction many times since Bex had joined Bond Team, but though they were now trusting team-mate close, they still hadn't quite made it to kissing in a darkened room close. Eddie doubted now that they ever would. Add Rebecca Deveraux to the ever-lengthening list of what-ifs and might-have-beens and look for someone new, he told himself. *Had* told himself, often. Trouble was his self just wouldn't listen.

And he'd missed quite a lot of what Deveraux was saying now, as well. Mention of his name had alerted him. 'Edward Nelligan, your region will be red. Therefore, your codename will be Edward Red.'

'Edward Red?' Eddie repeated. 'Could have been worse, I guess. Who'd have been up for Edward Puce?'

'And finally, Lori Angel, your region will be blue. Therefore, your codename will be Angel Blue.'

'How come Lori always gets the best codename?' Eddie grumbled.

'You will see your areas of operation and your placement bases identified on the map,' said Jonathan Deveraux.

The holographic map that spread suddenly from ceiling to floor and wall to wall was like a high-tech spider's web. It depicted all the countries of the world and was splashed with colour: realms of red, blue, white, green, black and orange, trickling along coastlines, sweeping across vast tracts of land, dabbing at islands and missing none of them out. The world divided into sections, each to be guarded and protected against any and every threat to peace and stability by its own dedicated Spy High agent. Certain cities were lit up, one in each colour, the cities which the graduates would be making their base of operations, where they would carve out their new lives and wait until it was necessary to call on all the expertise they'd developed at Deveraux.

Eddie scanned for the red. 'Let it be a nice tropical island somewhere. Or the west coast. I'd like California. Hollywood. San Francisco. LA. I can fit in there. I can do glamorous. Or the Caribbean. Anywhere with a decent beach. Red red red. Where are you?'

He found it. And nearly turned green.

'You're kidding me. You've got to be kidding me. Europa? A has-been continent. Nobody bothers going there any more, not even the bad guys. Anybody want to swap, my red for your, well, what colour have you got?'

'No swapping allowed, Eddie,' grinned Ben. 'This isn't the school playground. So where are you based?'

Eddie consulted the map again. His dismay was complete. 'Well, it's a place with plenty of past which is good, 'cause from what I've heard it's not got much of a future.' He sighed in full make-the-best-of-it mode. 'Look out, London. Here comes Edward Red.'

ONE

Two years later

They sat in a dimly lit room, the small, frightened-looking man and his companion, who was not at all small and who seemed far from frightened. They sat and they sipped from golden glasses of whisky as the night wore on. And they talked, in tones hushed with secrecy.

'You know the legend, I suppose,' said the small man. 'The legend of King Arthur? Of course you must.'

'I am familiar with it. Why?'

'The days of Camelot, when Arthur founded a fellowship of knights whose noble deeds and glorious achievements shine out to this very day. A proud nation united behind a gracious and gallant king. The righteous warriors of the Table Round—'

'I am *familiar* with it.'

'Of course. Of course you are.' The frightened-looking man smiled meekly in apology. 'If only we had lived in such a time,' he said, 'or if such a time could come again.'

'Dreams are for children and old men, Digby. We are neither.'

'But if I may remind you of the final fate of King Arthur,' pursued the small man. 'According to some tellings of the tale at any rate, when Camelot fell and ruin followed, as all great enterprises must ultimately come to an end, Arthur himself did not die. Not in the sense that we understand death. No, instead he passed into another place, some say an underground cavern where the good king and all his knights slumber and sleep, awaiting the hour when England has need of them again. Some say it is written there, 'Hic iacet Arthurus, rex quondam rexque futurus'. Which in English —'

'I am not a stranger to Latin. Some schools still have standards, Digby. The inscription allegedly reads "Here lies Arthur, the once and future king".'

'Indeed. Indeed.' The man called Digby squirmed uncomfortably on his seat. 'So you see –' uttering a nervous laugh – 'the legend does include the notion that one day a time of greatness for England will come again, most likely when her fortunes are at their direst and most desperate.'

'I begin to see your point, I think, Digby. But I also begin to tire of your company. Your remuneration is contingent upon the provision of information that is of *practical* use.'

Digby's plump fingers fluttered in the air like levitating sausages. 'Then let me take the liberty of fast-forwarding the centuries far beyond the age of Arthur Pendragon and pause in the middle of the last century. The 1950s. The height of the Cold War. Britain and our allies living in constant fear of the Communist

Bloc, the Soviet Union and *her* allies, dreading the threat of nuclear weapons and their possible deployment against a population with virtually no protection.'

'The good old days. Backs against the wall. A clear and present danger. Ancient history now, Digby.'

'But not then,' the small man pointed out. '*Then* it was the vital and all-consuming priority of the security services to combat the Soviet menace by whatever means necessary. My predecessors had many strange ideas, I can tell you. Most of them were never acted upon and are simply recorded in the kind of files deemed too sensitive ever to be made public. Like the name and details of the actor who became Churchill after his assassination in 1940. Scarcely anybody knows that these files even exist nowadays. They're stored in the lowliest of sub-basements at the Ministry to which only a handful of people have access, and as the files are composed of something as old-fashioned as paper, even those with a right to consult them think that to do so would be beneath their dignity. I can assure you that nobody else is aware of this but me.'

'Aware of *what*?'

'Of one very interesting Cold War plan that *was* put into practice. The Pendragon Project.'

'I'm listening.'

'What if the Russians attacked? What if their bombs rained from the skies and obliterated all our surface bases, wiped out our military capability, destroyed in one sweep our capacity to retaliate? It was a possible scenario, and my predecessors at the highest level decided that immediate steps should be taken to guard against such an eventuality. A huge underground complex was designed. It was to be self-sustaining. Life support systems, food and drink production, everything required for a society to survive and perpetuate itself, all was to be generated and controlled entirely from within the complex. The Pendragon Project was to be home to a colony of super-scientists, the greatest, most patriotic minds in the country, men and women who would be prepared to forego their lives on the surface for an existence far below ground, devoting their considerable mental resources to one end only. The creation of the most devastating and destructive weapons technologies that mankind had seen, weapons that would be ready for England to use in her hour of need.'

'So what happened?'

The small man seemed less frightened now. He could see the effect his words were having on his companion. 'The complex was built. Volunteers came forward. The scientists were taken underground and the Pendragon Project was sealed, you might say like a tomb. To focus the colony's mind on its work the Project was completely cut off from the surface. No access to news. No sense of the passing of time. No communication with the upper world of any kind. Deaths were faked where necessary to remove the danger of prying relatives. The workers who'd helped to construct the complex, the soldiers who'd escorted its residents there, every member of the security or civil services who had had anything to do with the Pendragon Project in any way, who might ever have heard the name, everyone except the Heads of MI5 and MI6 themselves, were brainwashed to forget all about it. Written records were supposed to be eradicated, too, but somehow the files survived. I suppose it was too much to expect total efficiency from the British Security Services, even then. The idea was that the Pendragon scientists were to be sleepers, like King Arthur and his knights, to be roused only when the Heads of MI5 and MI6 jointly thought it necessary, in who knew how many years ahead. The scientists in the colony could not at any point contact their political masters. Their orders were to wait for their superiors to contact *them*. Their sons and daughters are waiting still.'

'What do you mean, Digby?'

The small man was excited now, aware that his information was proving as valuable to his companion as he'd hoped. 'Times have changed here on the surface. Britain has changed. The Cold War is, as you say, ancient history, and those who authorized the Pendragon Project are long dead. Their successors may once have known of it but no more. Yet it exists. It is still there. For a hundred years now, a colony of scientists has been inventing undreamed-of weapons beneath England's green and pleasant land and for them *nothing has changed*. Who knows what secrets they might have discovered, what power they might be able to bestow? They wait to serve their country.' A momentary hesitation before the final gamble. 'They wait to serve *you*.'

'Where is this Pendragon Project to be found?'

'The files map its location.'

'And where are the files?'

'In a safe place, of course.' Digby uttered a little laugh and smiled ingratiatingly. 'I can fetch them. But first, we did discuss . . . remuneration?'

'Of course.' For the first time that evening, the small man's companion permitted himself a smile. It was reminiscent of a fox in a chicken coop. 'Once I have the files, Digby, you will receive what you deserve. I promise you that.'

IGC DATA-FILE 2066
SUB-SECTION: GREAT BRITAIN MEDIA FEED
Celebrities and local dignitaries will be among those attending the opening of the Stonehenge Shopping and Entertainment Mall today. The Mall, the largest in the South of England, has been built on and around the site of the ancient monument, the stones themselves now roofed over and forming the centrepiece of the attraction among a tasteful arrangement of waterfalls and fountains. Each stone has been freshly painted in vivid colours, in accordance with the Stonehenge Mall's slogan: 'There's Nothing Grey About Us'. The stones have also been stamped with the logos of their individual sponsors.

In other news, a new series of 'The Windsors' begins tonight on BBC 13, with the royal family still struggling to come to terms with their reduced circumstances and life in suburbia. 'The Windsors' has proven to be the most out-standingly successful example of reality videvision yet, and highlights of the new series will surely include Prince Darren's attempt to become a pop star by recording a cybertronic version of the country's new Multinational Anthem.

Finally, sport, and plans to mark the cente-nary of England's first and only winning of the

football World Cup with a series of celebratory
events are continuing apace. The highlight is
certain to be a holographic restaging of the
historic match between England and West Germany
where viewers can alter the outcome, the weather
conditions and even the identity of the players
at the flick of a switch. Meanwhile, England's
four remaining professional football sides have
confirmed that their players *will* attend a gala
charity event now that the matter of their fee
has been resolved.

Eddie's flat was in Camden Town, just north of London's famous West End Zone. It was an area of the city popular with young, well-heeled and rebellious types who came there to be fashionable drop-outs for a couple of years before taking up their position with Daddy's company or claiming their inheritance. Eddie's father owned no company and he could expect little by way of inheritance, but he too lived in Camden Town under slightly false pretences.

His flat, for example. It was on the top floor of a small block of purpose-built apartments, along with residences occupied by a Miss T Flynn, Mr and Mrs Harmer, and one Pete Dawes. Sadly for them, however, Miss T Flynn, Mr and Mrs Harmer and one Pete Dawes did not in fact exist – small wonder that they were never seen in the elevator or that their windows were always closed. In reality the four flats on the top floor were all one apartment, belonging to Edward Nelligan and purchased for him by the Deveraux College. It meant that as well as Eddie's normal living accommodation, there was room for one or two Spy High style embellishments, like a holo-gym, a lab and weapons maintenance centre, and a SkyBike bay.

'You know, it's funny when you think about it, isn't it, Bowler?' Eddie said. 'Nobody I meet having a clue what I really do, I mean. Nobody at work. Nobody downstairs guessing what's right above their heads. Maybe I should tell them, let them know that their freedom and security are in safe hands, what do you think?'

'I feel that would be what in my youth we would call a genuine rib-tickler, Master Edward, and the subsequent resources that Mr Deveraux would have to expend in mind-wiping half the population of Camden Town . . . most hilarious.' The speaker paused. 'Are you ready now for your morning work-out?'

'Absolutely, Bowler,' Eddie confirmed, clapping his hands together, 'and this time it's gonna be *you* ending up on your back.'

'Master Edward, truly, your humour knows no bounds.'

Eddie followed the man called Bowler into the holo-gym. He came with the territory, did Bowler. He was the Deveraux organisation's British liaison officer, part mentor, part operational adviser, part personal trainer, and all traditional English reserve. If his upper lip was any stiffer it would snap off whenever Bowler started to talk. Eddie liked to think of him as Alfred to his own Batman, an interpretation largely borne out by the man's appearance. Bowler *dressed* like a butler, impeccably pressed pin-stripe trousers, impossibly creaseless long dark frock-coat, wing-collared shirt as white as purity and a black tie knotted with such perfection that only a computer could have done it. Bowler *behaved* like a butler, impassive, undemonstrative, unfailingly deferential and polite, his expression always one of calm repose, perhaps the mildest of amused twinkles in his eye whenever he thought of Eddie. Only one thing marred the overall impression. Bowler certainly did not *fight* like a butler.

Eddie straightened the jacket of his judogi, tightened the belt. A little bit of the martial arts to start the day was never a bad idea. No need for a holo-program, either, not when Bowler was at hand. 'You're not going to change into a judogi, then, Bowler?' Eddie said.

'I'm sure that won't be necessary, Master Edward.' Bowler contented himself with removing his frock-coat and shoes, hung the former from the wall and placed the latter tidily beneath it.

'Bit unhygienic, though, isn't it?' Eddie goaded. 'You know, when you start to work up a sweat.'

Bowler smiled understandingly. 'Thank you for your concern, Master Edward, but the possibility of perspiration is, I feel, rather slim. Shall we begin?'

'Let's do it.' Eddie bowed to his opponent as custom dictated. 'Rei.'

'Rei, Master Edward,' Bowler reciprocated.

And then Eddie was at him with a leap and a kick. This time he wasn't going to embarrass himself. This time he was going to utilise his speed, his vigour, go straight for the jugular, so to speak. Bowler was thirty-plus years older than him. Eddie should be offering him his seat on public transport, not confronting him in the holo-gym. This time he was going to put the record straight.

The leap and the kick missed. Bowler had stepped aside with the manners of one making way for a lady.

Eddie landed, shifted his weight on to his right leg and pivoted to kick out with his left. Bowler swayed back to avoid it as if he had a spring for a spine.

Eddie switched tactics, trying some hand-moves, instead.

He launched what he would have described in an immodest moment as a crippling barrage of blows. Bowler fended them off almost apologetically, blocking each new strike with psychic precision. But wait. What was this? His defences seeming to drop? Eddie had already committed himself before the idea of a feint occurred to him. It didn't matter – as with consummate grace and economy Bowler took advantage of Eddie's impetuous blunder and threw him – he'd have plenty of time to reconsider tactics from the floor.

'How did you do that?' Eddie groaned. 'How did you *do* that?'

'If one told you,' Bowler said, inspecting his cufflinks, 'one would have to kill you.'

Eddie lay on his back but couldn't help laughing. 'One day, Bowler . . .'

'As you say, Master Edward, but perhaps for now you had better shower before you go to work?'

They called it work but to Eddie it was child's play. Whoever had decided on the cover stories for Bond Team back at Deveraux had obviously been on particularly ingenious form when it came to finding a surrogate career for him. Eddie had been a SkyBike champion in his youth, his SkyBiking record at Spy High was second to none, so what could be a more suitable occupation than a mechanic at a SkyBike centre? A member of a race team, Eddie had tried to suggest, but the idea was dismissed as being dangerously high profile. A bike demonstrator, then, and he could do it with some funny glasses on and a false moustache to keep incognito. The response was a variation on don't be ridiculous, Nelligan. He was supposed to stay in the background. He was supposed to keep his head down – literally – and so he was going to be a mechanic.

And to be fair, most days it wasn't too bad. Eddie quickly gained a reputation as the best young mechanic the North London SkyBike Centre had ever had, and he got to ride as well as service and repair the machines. So most days, everything went smoothly enough.

Today wasn't one of those days.

There was a lot of work on for a start, and Eddie seemed slower than usual about it, allowing himself to become distracted by possible ways of finally beating Bowler in the holo-gym.

'Thought you might have finished that Zero Mark Three by now.' His boss increased his woes as bosses always do.

'Sorry, Mr Clancey. Almost,' said Eddie. And did you know I could probably kill you in thirty different ways while standing on my head, he was tempted to add.

'Only the owner's going to be in for it later.'

'He sure is,' said Eddie. 'You'd better get the guy to sit down before you give him the bill. It's not gonna be one of his happier moments. The magnetic core was shot to pieces.'

'Well, get it done as quickly as you can. *Before* you break for lunch, Nelligan.'

'Goes without saying, Mr Clancey. Who needs food anyway when you're having this much fun?'

'There's no need for sarcasm. Don't think you're irreplaceable, Nelligan,' said Mr Clancey, though in his private moments he had to concede that Eddie pretty much *was*. 'I'm going out. See you later. With the Zero Mark Three good as new.'

But Eddie was still working on it when the owner arrived, and Clancey hadn't returned, either.

He heard them first, standing behind him in the entrance to the work bay. Three guys and one girl, all maybe a couple of years older than himself. Eddie didn't need to look up to learn what they were like. Psychoanalysis of speech tones and vocal inflections was one of the Personality Modules at Spy High. The snide whispers and superior chuckles from the boys as they watched him scarcely taxed his training. Basically, these guys' personalities sucked.

'Excuse me, did you want something?' At last Eddie stood and turned.

'He can speak. The grease monkey can speak,' sniggered one of the newcomers into another's ear.

'Actually, yes,' indicated the third male, curly-haired and with a nose that really required a larger face to fulfil its destiny. 'My Zero Mark Three. That's it behind you. I do hope you're not still slaving away on it.'

'Don't be too hard on the young man, Jules. I'm sure he's trying his best.' Apart from being distinguished from his companions by a rather silly name and a rather visible nose, Jules also stood out as the only one of the boys to come complete with girlfriend. A willowy brunette was kind of twisted around him, like ivy encircling an oak.

Eddie made a note. A very cute willowy brunette. And if she hadn't been there, and if Bowler hadn't thrown him this morning, and if he'd been a genuine career mechanic dependent upon the job rather than an impostor, Eddie might have resigned himself to an apology and a promise to finish the work as promptly as possible. But sometimes, keeping your head down just wasn't good enough. Sometimes, you had to lift it high.

' 'Fraid the bike'll be a while yet,' he said. ' 'Course, it would have helped if I hadn't had to replace the magnetic core with a new one.'

'A new one? Why?' Jules was not happy. He shook his girlfriend off. 'This was only supposed to be a routine service.'

'The old one had gone into terminal meltdown,' Eddie explained, not actually appearing too sad about it. 'Someone needs to stop over-revving the engine, or else someone needs to get used to paying out large sums of money for major repairs.'

The three boys gaped at the grease monkey's effrontery. Willowy Brunette regarded Eddie with new-found interest.

'You can't talk to me like that,' objected Jules. 'Do you know who I am? I could get you sacked from your crappy little job just like that.' He clicked his fingers as if summoning a waiter in a high-class restaurant.

'Maybe you could,' said Eddie, 'but it wouldn't make you a better SkyBiker.'

'No? I suppose you think you know one or two things about riding SkyBikes, grease monkey.'

'One or two,' Eddie admitted modestly.

Jules had perhaps expected a different response. 'Yes, well, we'll soon see —'

'Are you going to race him, Julesy?' Willowy Brunette clung even more closely to him, fluttering her lashes like they were fans to cool his blood. 'Go on. Race him. For me. You know how I like it when you go *fast*.'

'I *would*, Bella,' Jules claimed boldly. 'Let me assure you, nothing would give me greater pleasure than to put this impudent *mechanic* in his place.' A note of regret, not altogether sincere, crept into his voice. 'But baby, neither of us has a bike.'

'Actually, mine's outside,' said Eddie.

'It's not that old Mark One we saw, is it?' said one of Jules's friends. It was – part of Eddie's low profile. 'That ought to be in a *museum*. You can borrow my Mark Three, Jules. He won't have a chance.'

'Then we're set!' Willowy Brunette peeled herself away from Jules and clapped well-manicured hands. 'A race. Jules versus the grease monkey. That is – ' and here she aimed her mobile eyelashes at Eddie–'if you're man enough to take him on.'

'Actually, I do have work to do . . .' What was the girl playing at? She was deliberately goading both of them.

'Not if Jules complains to your boss,' she countered. 'So you've no choice. You have to race. If Jules wins, he loses you your job. If you win . . .' She considered coyly. 'Well, I'm sure we can come up with some kind of prize . . .'

Eddie sighed. He had no doubt that this Jules was influential enough to get him fired, and unemployment was not part of his cover story. Seemed Willowy Brunette was right about his lack of options. 'Okay, you've got it. I'm in.'

'Excellent.' Jules himself was bolstered by the availability of a Mark Three. 'So where and when?'

'You must have a SkyTrack somewhere for testing, mustn't you?' Bella was pushing on again. 'What about there? And I don't see anyone who looks like management around. So why wait? What about *now*?'

The girl in fact appeared the most excited member of the group as they made their way outside to the SkyTrack at the rear of the centre. Eddie made another note. Cute but manipulative. Just the kind he'd always been taught to avoid – not by Deveraux but by his mother. His old mum wasn't around just at the moment, though, so when Bella fixed him with her bright, mischievous stare, he stared back.

The SkyTrack resembled an athletics track, circular and laned, only the lanes were marked out by beams of light instead of paint and were located ten metres up in the air. The height was adjustable, depending on the testing procedure to be carried out. For a straightforward test of speed, 'Ten metres is fine,' said Jules. 'Or does the grease monkey want it lowered? That crate of his doesn't look like it'll get off the ground.'

The confidence born of the prospect of riding a superior machine was swiftly turning into arrogance as Jules watched Eddie prepare his battered Zero Mark One. The essential design of the SkyBikes was the same, the saddle and the chassis modelled on old petrol-driven motorbikes, though sleeker and more streamlined, the magnetic engine or core protruding

bulbously from the front of the vehicle with the twin
and circular propulsion units on either side of the bike
at the back. The difference between the Mark One and
the Mark Three models lay in the latter's significantly
increased powers of acceleration and sustained speed:
propulsion unit technology had made major advances
over the past few years.

The hare and the tortoise, Eddie thought. And while
Jules was unlikely to stop mid-race for a nap, he, Eddie,
was one heck of a tortoise.

'A practice lap just to warm up the bikes,' Bella
ruled, 'then six laps to the finish. And may the best *man*
win.'

'I will do, baby. Don't worry.' Jules squeezed her, kind
of slobbered over her for morale.

And Bella let him. 'I won't worry,' she said. 'I won't
worry at all.' But her eyes were on Eddie.

They activated their cores and let the magnetic power
of their bikes lift them easily into the air. Eddie knew
he'd be coming from behind, which meant he'd have to
convert drawback into advantage. He trusted himself to
wring every last drop of power out of his bike that it pos-
sessed. Over short distances, the Mark One ought to be
able to match the Mark Three. It was all going to be a
matter of timing.

'Go!' yelled Bella.

They went.

And Jules was over-revving already, Eddie could
hear it. He did spurt into the predictable early lead,
however, and even found time to glance behind him in
jeering disdain.

Hare and tortoise.

Eddie didn't try to overtake. He slotted in behind Jules's machine, raced in his slipstream. Let the Mark Three do all the work. Conserve his more limited resources for later.

Lap One. Lap Two. By the halfway point Jules was finding Eddie's presence directly to his rear a matter of irritation. He couldn't shake him off. If they'd been racing over open country it might have been different, but on a SkyTrack there were bends to negotiate as well as straights, and he had to curb his speed a little or he'd be hurtling into the safety zone.

'Come on! Faster!' screamed Bella. 'You can do it!' She didn't specify who.

Lap Four. Lap Five. Eddie made his move. He swung wide off a bend and gunned the core with everything he had. His propulsion units blazed, whirled madly. His body was jolted back as the bike accelerated. He and Jules were neck and neck. The could have reached out to shake hands, or to do something more violent to each other, which was likelier. There was outrage and shock on the rich boy's face.

Eddie swept into a lead, slotted directly in front of the Mark Three, giving Jules time to reconsider his own tactics.

'He's gone too early!' Bella cried. 'Jules can overtake him!' But even psychoanalysis of speech tones and vocal inflections would have been hard-pressed to decide whether this likelihood inspired or appalled her.

They began the final lap.

He'll do the same as me, Eddie wagered. He'll try an identical manoeuvre coming off the bend into the back straight. It'll have to be then to give him time to overtake.

Which was just as well. Eddie's instruments showed that the Mark One could sustain such velocities for only seconds longer or risk core-seizure. To overhaul him, the Mark Three would have to be seriously speeding.

The bend. Jules swung wide. Over-revved like a madman. Shot past Eddie with a howl of what he thought was going to be imminent victory. But why was the grease monkey's bike actually *slowing*? The final bend. He'd need to slow too. He was going too fast. If he couldn't, if he didn't, if he . . .

His howl attained a pitch more associated with defeat than victory.

The Mark Three's acceleration was hot. Its braking took a while.

Jules's SkyBike shot off the track entirely. Its systems were neutralised as soon as it entered the safety zone. It thudded heavily to earth, scratches in the paint-work. The suspension was going to need attention, too. Jules's friend who'd loaned him the bike looked like he might soon be redefining the nature of their relationship.

Eddie's features, however, denoted quiet satisfaction. It wasn't hard to win a race when you were the sole remaining competitor, even if your SkyBike was a bit wobbly after its recent exertions.

'So,' said Bella when he'd returned to ground, 'you've still got a job, then.'

'Looks like it.' Eddie sauntered over to Jules and his companions. 'Thanks for the race.' He looked down at the damaged Mark Three and tutted. 'By the way, if you want to book this in for repairs I can probably fit it in tomorrow. Just got to finish some work on another bike first. Same model, funnily enough. Owner's supposed to be in for it later.' He allowed himself a grin. 'Guess I'll see you then, Jules.'

'Not if I see you first, grease monkey,' grumbled Jules, but he cut an unimpressive figure now and nobody seemed to be listening to him. 'Let's go, Bella.'

'You go. I'll see you later. Maybe.' In an undertone. And after she'd pursued Eddie back inside to the work bays.

'Not leaving with your boyfriend?' Eddie said. Third note. Cute, manipulative and disloyal. Where was a ten foot bargepole when he needed one?

'Who, Jules?' She seemed to smell something bad. 'He's no-one special. You proved that just now. So, do mechanics have names?'

'Eddie.'

'All of them or just you?'

'Just me.'

'That's good. Because it's just you I'm interested in. Eddie.'

'Is that right?'

'Exactly right. You beat Jules fair and square so it's nearly time for your prize.'

'*Nearly* time?'

'I don't like to eat dinner before eight. Here, Eddie.' Bella scribbled a number on a piece of paper and handed it to him. 'Call me. And take a nap when you get home. I like to stay out late.'

'Thanks for the advice.' He'd memorised Bella's number already. Spy High memory training had so many wonderful applications. He grinned to himself. Things were looking up.

IGC DATA-FILE 2066
SUB-SECTION: GREAT BRITAIN MEDIA FEED

A body recovered from the Thames yesterday has been identified as that of Charles Digby, a civil servant in the Ministry of Defence. Mr Digby was last seen several days ago and was reported missing by his wife. Police are not looking for anyone in connection with the death.

TWO

'I told you this was a bad idea,' said old Mrs Kenyon, 'but do you listen to me? No. As soon as you start drawing a pension it's as if your opinion no longer counts. But why should I be surprised? You've always been a wilful boy, Robert, ever since —'

'Thank you, Mother,' sighed Mr Robert Kenyon, her son. 'I think we know how you feel but I promise once we get *on* to the bridge the traffic'll start moving again.'

'Why don't you read your magazine, dear?' suggested Kay Kenyon, Robert's wife. 'Or try a spot of knitting to help you relax?'

'Look out the window, Gran!' bounced their son James next to his Grandma. 'You can see it. You can see the bridge from here!'

And he was right. They were close enough to the White Cliffs Terminal now to gain their first glimpse of the Channel Bridge itself. There it was in all its glittering glory, stretching out from the coast of England to the coast of France, spanning a watery gulf of more than twenty miles' width like a rainbow, only not quite as arched, not quite as colourful, and with huge steel and concrete pillars plunged into the sea every hundred metres or so to support the structure. One of the greatest feats of engineering of the twenty-first century.

If only the queues weren't so long to pay the toll.

'Of course, the true value of the bridge is symbolic,' said Kay Kenyon. 'It's visible evidence that Britain is part of Europa. The tunnel served a similar purpose, I know, but that was underground, you couldn't *see* it. It was like we were ashamed to show it, to acknowledge what it meant, but not with the bridge. Nobody can mistake what the bridge means. Britain's future lies with Europa.'

'Does she always talk that kind of nonsense, Robert?' said old Mrs Kenyon. 'I told you you should have married that nice Evie Thatcher girl, but do you listen to me? No. And you should listen to nice Mr Knight, too. *He* knows what he's talking about. If God hadn't meant Britain to be an island, He wouldn't have surrounded us with sea.'

'Oh, how ridiculous,' scoffed Mrs Kenyon's daughter-in-law. 'Robert, I told you we should have left her in the home. Your mother's not a good influence on James. She's not *modern*.'

'Gran, look!' James was bubbling, pressing his nose against the wheelless' window and plucking at his Grandma's sleeve. 'We're there!'

Robert slotted credits into the auto-toll, a green light winked as if drivers and bridge were all pals together, and then the Kenyons were edging out beyond the last land of Britain. Below their wheelless was their allocated lane in the Europa-bound section of the Channel Bridge, and below that nothing but a yawning chasm to the churning waters of the Channel itself. James had insisted on his dad queueing for Lane One so that he'd have a better view of the sea.

'Wow, Gran, isn't this great?' If it wasn't the rule that vehicles' windows had to remain closed, the boy would have had his head and half his body thrust out over the side by now.

'This is a bad idea,' grumbled Mrs Kenyon. 'The bridge is swaying. I'm sure I can feel it swaying. I told you we should have gone to Bournemouth as usual, but do you listen to me? No.'

'Mother, the bridge is perfectly safe,' calmed Robert Kenyon. 'It's the most safety-conscious bridge ever designed. Nothing can go wrong.'

'Dad,' said James, 'what's that cloud?'

'Cloud, son?' Not wanting to take his eyes off the road, Robert Kenyon merely glanced to the left where James was indicating. The sky *had* been perfectly clear, like somebody had just cleaned it. Now it wasn't. The cleaner had missed a smudge after all. 'Clouds are clouds, aren't they? And don't worry, when it rains the bridge's retractable roof . . .'

'But it's coming closer, Dad.'

The boy was no longer gazing captivated at the sea. Instead he was transfixed by a dark mass in the sky that did indeed look rather like a cloud, but one that was moving so fast and so purposefully that it evidently had serious business to attend to. And from the direction of its path, that business had something to do with the Channel Bridge.

'He's right, Robert,' said Kay Kenyon. 'It's heading straight for us.'

'And Mum,' James added, 'what's that noise?'

'I told you this was a bad idea.'

A humming. A droning. Like a swarm of bees or wasps, insects that sting. Coming from the cloud that was a swathe of blackness now and swooping unerringly towards the bridge. Easily heard above the smooth magnetic engines of the wheellesses. Growing louder, more ominous.

'I think you'd better sit back down properly now, James,' said Robert Kenyon. He looked nervously to his right. You weren't supposed to change lanes on the bridge – its entire length was monitored and doing so would earn you an automatic fine at the other end – but all of a sudden Robert Kenyon was beginning to feel that he'd sooner *be* at the other end, fined or not, safely on solid ground again rather than balancing on this thin ribbon of road raised high above the sea. Lane Two seemed to be moving more quickly, though most of its vehicles' occupants were also pointing and staring at the dark cloud approaching.

Which suddenly seemed to explode. No boom of detonation, no flash of fire, but the single shape shattered nonetheless, broke up into innumerable smaller pieces, the fragments flying still towards the bridge. Towards the vehicles upon it. Drawn like predators to the smell of blood.

'Dad, what are they?' James chilled, his excitement forgotten.

Metal spheres with four sharp prongs projecting from them, like claws flexing for something to sink into. The spheres buzzing, hunting.

'Doodle-bugs,' said old Mrs Kenyon. 'My Nanna used

to tell me about them. In the war. Hitler sent them over. Doodle-bugs. Bombs. I told you we should have gone to Bournemouth.'

'*Bombs?*' Kay Kenyon was about to say that was impossible. Events contradicted her.

The first wave dipped low and slammed into the side of the bridge. Their blast caused the structure to do more than sway. It shuddered, badly jolted by the shells' destructive force. There were cracks in the concrete.

To hell with a fine, Robert Kenyon decided as plumes of smoke and flame billowed from the bridge to their left. They could take his life savings if they wanted to, just as long as he *had* a life. He steered frantically into Lane Two.

Unfortunately, everybody else in the Kenyons' lane had the same idea at the same time. Inevitable result: chaos. In the crunch and the collision of vehicles, people were screaming.

The second wave of bombs didn't exactly help.

They whirled towards their targets, not randomly, not by accident, shrilly shrieking at such close range. Guided. Directed. A fatal attraction.

The wheelless ahead of the Kenyons, the wheelless behind. Concertinaed together in the crash, engines dead. Two shells smashed into their roofs, their spikes stabbing into the metal, activating detonators. The explosive force sent the two vehicles leaping into the air and splintered every window in the Kenyons' wheelless.

'Out! Out!' Robert Kenyon was crying. A third bomb was careering unstoppably towards them.

The family spilled on to the bridge, stayed low as their car erupted behind them. The shells swarmed above, seeming suddenly to lock on to a victim and then home in with frightening accuracy.

And now their incessant buzzing was not the only noise to terrify the hapless travellers trapped on the bridge. The concrete was crumbling with a sound like a distant avalanche. Cracks appeared in the road like wrinkles in an old man's face. The Channel Bridge, one of the greatest feats of engineering of the twenty-first century, was unlikely to make the twenty-second.

'It's just like my Nanna told me about the war,' said Mrs Kenyon, almost approvingly.

'Doesn't she ever shut *up*?' wailed Kay Kenyon, sprawling in the midst of carnage.

'I told you, Robert,' old Mrs Kenyon scolded, the bridge a river of fire. 'I told you this was a bad idea.'

Ninety per cent of accidents happen at home. Eddie was familiar with the statistic. In a secret agent's home he'd always imagined the tally would be closer to the full hundred.

You had to be so careful. Did you leave the shock-mat in the hall energised or not energised when you went out? Did you remember to switch on/off your rooms' automatic defence systems as appropriate? Did you absolutely commit to memory the personalised nine digit code of your Last Resort Home-Self-Destruct Sequence? It was all so much more complicated than simply checking your electrical fittings and being mindful what you did with boiling water.

Even here in the bathroom. As Eddie tried for the umpteenth time to comb his unruly red hair into some kind of impressive order for his date with Bella, he cast his eye over his wash-basin. Toothbrush: best to clean your teeth with the one that wasn't in reality a radio transmitter and could fire a laser beam in its spare time. Toothpaste: use the brand that tasted of mint and not of plastic explosive, or that pearly white smile might become a bit of a problem. Shaving foam: the one with the cream, not the gas. And never drop the soap, just to be on the safe side: holes in the bathroom floor were always a little difficult to explain away.

He sort of hoped Bella wouldn't want to visit. Maybe she'd invite him to her place . . .

Not that he should think that far ahead. You had to approach a date like you would a mission (with the possible exception of parachuting into the restaurant): take nothing for granted and be prepared for all possible eventualities. Of course, he could improve his chances with Bella by fitting his Spy High issue auto-suggestion contact lenses, but to try to control her mind artificially like that would be an unforgivable infringement of her human rights as well as the cowardly act of a hopeless loser unable to form healthy relationships on his own.

Maybe he'd try that on the second date.

'Oh, most presentable, Master Edward,' acknowledged Bowler when Eddie finally emerged ready for the evening. 'Of course, in my day we tended not to go in for jackets that were *quite* so yellow or, indeed, for trousers that were quite so green, but at least your young lady will be able to see you across a crowded room.' Bowler considered. 'Or two.'

'Haven't you got a home to go to, Bowler?' Eddie wanted to know.

'Ah, just finishing polishing your footwear, Master Edward.' The liaison officer presented Eddie with a sparkling pair of black boots by way of proof.

'Thanks, but I don't think I'll be needing those tonight.'

'Oh, of course not, Master Edward,' said Bowler. 'These are not for casual wear. They form part of the latest consignment of operatives' clothing from Deveraux.'

'The secret agent's autumn collection, right?'

'Treated with the same adhesive substance as clingskin, I understand.'

'Yeah? Well it's a pity I can't stick around for you to tell me more, Bowler, but I've got a hot babe waiting for me and I don't want to disappoint her.'

'How could you possibly do that, Master Edward?'

Eddie snorted. 'I'll probably find a way somehow.' He turned towards the door, paused, turned back to Bowler. 'You know, Bowler, I know this is going to be difficult for you to believe, but I haven't always had a lot of luck with the opposite sex.'

'Really, Master Edward?' Bowler raised his eyebrows politely. 'I *am* surprised.'

'No, it's true. I'm sorry to have to admit it but . . . Bowler, not one of the girls in my team at Spy High ever really fell for me, not really. I mean, what's the problem? I don't have three heads, do I? I don't have a personal hygiene issue I don't know about, do I? Where am I going wrong?'

'Perhaps it's just that you haven't yet met the *right* girl, Master Edward,' Bowler theorised.

'But how am I supposed to *know* who's the right girl or

not? When the bad guys come along, they're easy to recognise. They're the ones trying to take over the world. But the right girl? Maybe she ought to have my name tattooed across her forehead. Tastefully done, mind.'

'You'll know, Master Edward,' said Bowler. 'When you do meet her, you'll know.'

'Yeah?' Eddie grinned, winked. 'Is this the voice of experience speaking Bowler? Is that a twinkle in the eye for Mrs Bowler, is it?'

'I do apologise, Master Edward,' the older man observed, 'but did you not a moment ago mention a certain young lady with a high temperature who is expecting your arrival?'

'You're right.' Eddie owned up. 'I'd better go. Turn on the defence systems when you leave, won't you, Bowler? See you tomorrow.'

'Indeed, Master Edward,' said Bowler, before adding a judicious: 'And good luck.'

IGC DATA-FILE 2066
SUB-SECTION: GREAT BRITAIN MEDIA FEED

The annual march of the Daughters of Diana will take place next week along the accustomed route to commemorate the 69th anniversary of her death. The event seems to grow in stature and popularity every year, and whereas in the early decades the marchers tended only to wear masks, in recent times advances in facial remodelling techniques, coupled with increased affordability, has led to many hundreds of the group's members physically transforming their appearance in homage to the late Princess of Wales. As usual, all money raised will go to charity.

Turning to politics, and controversy continues to rage over next month's Treaty of Europa Conference, to be held in London's Millennium Halls. While the Prime Minister has again assured the country that the conference is 'a consultative exercise only' and that 'no decision on Britain's future in Europa will be made without the people having their say', Bartholomew Knight, leader of the UK First Party is more sceptical. 'This conference is a charade and our signature to the Treaty of Europa a fait accompli,' he said. 'Promises have been made and the deal has been done. By the end of the year, the United Kingdom as we have known it for over a thousand years will have ceased to exist. I urge the people now to make their voices heard in protest before they are silenced forever.'

We interrupt this bulletin to bring you some breaking news. Reports are coming in of a possible terrorist outrage on the Channel Bridge. We are hearing that a number of massive explosions have torn through the structure and that its central section has collapsed into the sea. The bridge was crowded with people heading to and from Europa, many of whom are now feared dead. We will keep you updated on this story as it unfolds.

At Spy High, Eddie had once held his breath underwater without any artificial aids for nearly two and a half

minutes. It had been part of their training for survival in
hostile environments. Only Ben had actually beaten his
time, and Eddie had never been sure that that really
counted, bearing in mind that Ben would probably have
sooner drowned than finish second, particularly to him.
But anyway, he'd done it. One hundred and thirty-nine
seconds without coming up for air.

The way Bella was smothering him now, he was glad
of the practice.

'Oh, Eddie, you're a great kisser.' Bella finally broke
away.

One hundred and eleven seconds. Nearly.

'You're not so bad yourself,' Eddie gasped.

'It's the implants I had done last year,' said Bella
proudly. 'They increase the lips' suction power and keep
them plump and moist twenty-four hours a day.'

'Really? That's –' he hadn't noticed before, but Bella's
lips *did* bear a rather unsettling resemblance to twin red
caterpillars – 'very very nice.'

'You want more?' She leaned towards him again.

'Uh, what if we talk a bit first?' Eddie was vaguely
aware that he was kind of pinned into the corner of the
club. The bar, the dance floor and the flashing lights
seemed a long way away. And he couldn't see anything
tattooed across Bella's forehead, tastefully or otherwise.

'Talk? Talk's for old men and professors. What do you
want to talk about?'

'Well, I don't know,' Eddie blustered. 'Whatever you
like. You. The music you're into. The movies. Likes and
dislikes kind of thing.'

'Sounds like a job interview,' Bella disapproved. 'But

if we must. I *don't* like talking. I *do* like kissing. So shut up and kiss.'

One hundred and fifty-four seconds. Ben would have been proud.

They emerged from the club in the early hours of the morning. Not surprisingly, even with her wrap and Eddie's arm around her, Bella shivered with cold. Eddie hailed a SkyCab. One dipped low and hovered in front of them like a metal bird. After decades of relatively unchanging design, since the 2050s London's famous black cabs had undergone something of a makeover: the shell of a traditional taxi cab supplemented by a magnetic propulsion system similar to a SkyBike's. Hop aboard and you could be soaring above the rooftops of London. An impressive way to end a date.

Eddie helped Bella inside, closed the door behind him.

'Where to, guv'nor?' asked the cloth-capped and slouching cabbie without turning round. Bella told him her address. 'Right you are, Miss. I know it well. 'Old on an' 'ere we go.'

The cab rose into the sky.

'If this guy starts singing "The Lambeth Walk",' Eddie shared with Bella, 'I think we should get out.'

'I'm not getting out until we get home,' said Bella. But she was wrong.

The floor opened up beneath her feet. Her seat tipped forward. Bella fell through the bottom of the cab and it was already a *long* way down.

'My God!' cried Eddie.

But Bella wasn't plummeting. She was *floating*, buoyed up by a tractor beam that had been activated from under the cab and that was gently, carefully lowering her to the street. She wouldn't even stub a toe.

'What?' Eddie's attention snapped to the cabbie. He braced himself for an attack.

'I must apologise for disturbing your evening, Master Edward,' came a suddenly familiar voice from the front of the cab, 'but I'm afraid it was a matter of priorities.'

'*Bowler?*' He should have guessed.

'Indeed. Apparently there is, to paraphrase a favourite old saying from this part of the world, no cessation of work for the morally reprehensible.'

'But what about Bella?' Eddie peered through the hole in the floor. He could see her landing safely before the light of the tractor beam was extinguished.

'One of my colleagues is waiting for her at her home,' said Bowler. 'A little mind-wiping and she'll not remember anything about her journey home.'

The hatch in the cab's floor closed and they were moving again.

'You want to retro that mind-wipe a little further?' said Eddie. 'Like maybe to before our date started?'

'Was your evening not enjoyable, Master Edward?'

Eddie sighed faintly. 'Put it this way, Bowler. She's not the one.'

'Well, I'm afraid you would not have been seeing much more of the young lady in the immediate future in any case, Master Edward, not that there seemed much more of her *to* see.' Bowler's tone became even more grave than usual. 'Might I draw your attention to the screen, please.'

The glass screen between cabbie and fares flickered into a new life as a videvision monitor. Eddie forgot

about Bella as the voice of Jonathan Deveraux provided
an explanatory commentary to footage of the Channel
Bridge's assault by the swarm-shells. The sight of ruth-
less, rampant destruction and innocent people dying
always tended to focus Eddie's mind.

'An established terrorist group called Albion has
already claimed responsibility for the attack,' Jonathan
Deveraux was saying, 'but our own sources have yet to
verify this. A Deveraux operative must learn precisely
who *did* engineer this outrage and put an end to them by
whatever means necessary before they can strike again.
That is the mission.'

Eddie knew what was coming next. He *wanted* it to be
coming next.

'Edward Red, you have been assigned.'

THREE

'**S**o this is Europa?'

Eddie parted the clouds with his hands and bent lower to get a better view. Rivers and fields and towns and cities surrounded his feet and spread out in all directions, mountains scraped his shins. In the distance, the Mediterranean like a paddling pool.

'I know they say the world's getting smaller, but this is ridiculous. I don't think I dare move, Bowler. What if I step on Paris or Berlin by mistake and start an international incident?'

'Master Edward,' said Bowler with infinite patience, striding up the Appenines to join him, 'you are as aware as I am that this is a virtual topographical display of Europa designed for educational purposes. Might it be possible, therefore, to continue with the briefing?'

'Sure. Of course. Sorry.' Eddie looked suitably abashed.

'Then in answer to your question, yes, this is Europa. Once it was known as the Continent of Europe and consisted of a number of autonomous sovereign nation-states.

Germany. France. Italy. Now that is no longer the case. The Great Contamination of the 2020s —'

'Don't tell me,' interrupted Eddie. 'I remember this one from school. One of my old team-mates was a Domer, see, and the Domes were built because of the Great Contamination, weren't they? To protect what was left of the corn belt. After pollution almost wiped out food production in the 2020s.'

'Indeed,' said Bowler. 'To the widespread social unrest and political instability caused by the Great Contamination, the countries of the world responded in different ways. In Europa, where many nations were already part of a European Community, a radical proposal was accepted by most governments. To pool their resources and to secure their way of life before an unknown and uncertain future, individual countries were abolished. Germany, France, Italy and others, from the Eastern borders of what were once Poland and Hungary to the coastlines of the former Spain and Portugal, all ceased to exist. For the past thirty years and more there has only been Europa.'

'Bigger is better, huh?' Eddie followed Bowler north, stepping over minor territories once known as Holland and Belgium. 'I've heard that. But you said *most* governments. So Europa wasn't welcomed with open arms everywhere?'

'Indeed not,' said Bowler, pausing on the northern coast of France. 'Some countries refused to join Europa, the most prominent among them being my own.'

'Great Britain. Now I'm beginning to see the point of the history lesson.' He regarded the modestly-sized island from the shores of Europa. In comparison, it didn't look much. 'So what was the problem?'

'The British people have a long tradition of standing alone in moments of world crisis,' said Bowler, 'and in many ways a deep suspicion of the motives of their continental neighbours. Island races can so easily develop a siege mentality. And of course, there are many who would hate to abandon for all time the British flag, the British identity, the country's independence, even for what many considered to be a greater good . . .'

'So the Brits told Europa where to go, right?'

'Vigorously put, Master Edward,' Bowler said, 'but only partially accurate. For the last three decades there has existed an unbridgeable and intensifying division in this country between those who wish to join Europa with all expedition and those who would resist such a union to the last atom of their strength.'

The Europan landscape beneath their feet faded away. They were in a white place that cast no shadows, and they were accompanied by two men Eddie had seen on the news.

'Hullo,' said the first, bright-eyed and ruddy-cheeked like a schoolboy keen to make a good impression. 'I'm Perry Barnes. What do you believe in? Do you? So do I.'

'The Prime Minister of Great Britain,' introduced Bowler. 'The Right Honourable Peregrine Barnes QC. And the Foreign Secretary, the Right Honourable Damian Glover.'

The holographic representation of Glover did not speak or offer a pink palm in hopeful amity. He kept his hands behind his back where they couldn't be seen, and his heavily lidded eyes, underscored by deep grooves possibly rendered in ink, darted from side to side in a manner an opposition MP would be quick to describe as furtive.

'The principal proponents of the Europa Now Coalition,' said Bowler. 'The present government very much believes it's in Britain's interests to join. There's to be a conference held here in London in a few weeks, chaired by the Prime Minister and to which key members of the Europan administration have been invited. The idea is to finally dispel what Mr Barnes has called the damaging myths of what Europan membership might mean for the country which have been circulated by his opponents. He wants to publicise the true benefits. It's widely believed that a possible timetable for membership might also be discussed, prior to approval by the British people. One key figure who certainly won't be attending, however, is this man. Bartholomew Knight.'

A third hologram joined them. Physically, Bartholomew Knight was more impressive than both the Prime Minister and the Foreign Secretary, despite being in probably his late fifties and therefore a decade or so older than either. He was taller, broader, his hair thicker and more lustrous, his eyes steely points of determination. Eddie could imagine he didn't tolerate fools lightly and was used to getting his own way.

'Mr Knight founded and leads the main political party opposed to Europan membership, Master Edward,' said Bowler. 'The UK First Party. He's been accused of condoning the more extreme methods and opinions adopted by some groups, and even of secretly sponsoring them, though he is on record declaring that, while he will resist any movement towards increased Europan integration with all legal and political means at his disposal, he does not support and never has supported the use of violence.'

'I'm pleased to hear it,' said Eddie, 'particularly as we can always take a politician at his word.'

'Others,' continued Bowler, 'have not made the same pledge.'

Suddenly he and Eddie were encircled by malignant figures oozing menace and violence like sweat. They were all young, male and shaven-headed, booted and bomber-jacketed, with eyes like flints sparking to start a fire. Perry Barnes, Damian Glover and even Bartholomew Knight had vanished. Eddie thought they probably had the right idea.

'Meet the Jacks, Master Edward,' said Bowler.

'If it's all the same with you, Bowler, I'd rather not, thanks,' winced Eddie. 'I bet they're more imaginative when it comes to picking fights than they are when choosing names, right?'

'Oh, they call themselves Jacks after the traditional name for the flag of Great Britain, the Union Jack,' Bowler explained.

'Any particular reason why?'

'You'll see, Master Edward.'

The Jacks seemed to grow more agitated and angry. Their fists punched at the air as if they might draw blood. Their mouths spewed forth a torrent of hate couched in language that made Eddie blush even if Bowler remained his usual imperturbable self. But maybe the Jacks weren't as hardened to obscenity as their general demeanour suggested, anyhow. Their own cheeks seemed to be colouring. But not just red. Red, white and blue.

'I don't believe it,' gaped Eddie. As the Union Flag took up residence across the features of each and every Jack.

'Indeed,' observed Bowler. 'Before he is permitted to join the group, an aspiring Jack must voluntarily undergo facial repigmentation. He must become the flag to the extent that his alleged love for his country removes from him all trace of his own individuality.' Eddie saw what Bowler meant. The faces of the Jacks, distinctions smothered by the pattern and paint of the flags, were now identical. 'The surgical grafts responsible for the flag effects are connected to the centres of the brain that control human emotions,' Bowler continued. 'In short, only certain emotional stimuli trigger the appearance of the pigments. It would not be sensible for a Jack to be identifiable as such all the time.'

'So what are you saying?' pressed Eddie. 'They get mad and then they get flagged?'

'Indeed, Master Edward. Quaintly put.'

'Well at least you'll be able to see them coming,' Eddie said. 'What's the rest of the story? Thugs masquerading as patriots?'

'Effectively, yes. There are Jack cells in most major towns and cities, I am afraid, though we have not been able to establish whether they have a central leadership as yet. They claim to be a political organisation protesting against possible British membership of Europa.'

'And I'm betting those protests aren't peaceful, right?'

'Most intuitive, Master Edward. But the Jacks are at worst only a minor annoyance. Albion, on the other hand, is potentially a different proposition altogether.'

'Albion,' said Eddie. 'An old name for England, right?

And now it's what – the Armed League for British Independence as One Nation. Terrorists calling themselves freedom-fighters. Killers claiming a cause.'

'You are impressively well-informed, Master Edward,' acknowledged Bowler.

'I spent last night looking at the tapes of the Channel Bridge again. Couldn't sleep.' Eddie's expression twisted into an uncustomary glare. 'Couldn't sleep afterwards, either. Let's assume Albion are responsible for the atrocity as they claim. Why did they do it? Because they don't like the idea of Britain being connected to Europa? To make a point? Well, I'd say that anyone who thinks that murdering innocent people is a valid way to make a point needs to be spending the rest of their lives in a penal satellite reconsidering. So what say we bring the briefing to a close and get this mission on the road.'

Deveraux's contacts in the British intelligence services had managed to acquire some fragments of the swarm-shells from the Channel Bridge; a forensics team were trying to extract a lead from the charred and twisted metal casings. In the meantime, Eddie was on his way to the East End Zone to spend the evening in the company of the zealots of the UK First Party. Mr Bartholomew Knight would be addressing a public meeting off the Whitechapel Road.

Eddie thought it might be wise to learn a little more about Knight. For Albion to stage an attack as devastating as the one on the bridge, they had to have powerful and wealthy backers. Bartholomew Knight qualified under both headings and was also certainly in agreement with Albion's alleged *ends*, if not the means. He seemed to own half the country as it was. Probably why he didn't want the Europans getting their hands on it.

Eddie's cab – a basic model wheelless this time, and not driven by anyone even remotely associated with Spy High – idled at the Security checkpoint while both the cabbie's and Eddie's ID cards were checked by a police officer. The London of 2066 was pretty much split into two. In the West End Zone technology ruled. Many of the old buildings had been razed to the ground and gleaming new pinnacles to progress had been built in their place. There, the talk was not of *whether* Great Britain should become part of Europa, but *when*. Journey east, however, and it was like travelling back in time. Prosperity and the twenty-first century in general seemed to have passed the East End Zone by, as someone might cross the road to avoid a beggar. No new buildings here, no grand showpiece reconstruction programmes, just urban decay, dilapidation, dark and dangerous streets cordoned off from the outside world, prowled by predators like the Jacks and lived in by an aging and abandoned population who had nowhere else to go. It was a fertile recruiting ground for UK First.

'Okay. In you go,' said the cop, in a tone which seemed to question the mental health of anyone who would actively choose to proceed.

Eddie could see why. The cab took him through a bleak and badly-lit labyrinth, where shadows seemed to have a life of their own and sometimes followed and sometimes darted in front of the wheelless, where buildings closed in around the newcomers like gangs, and where drunks and derelicts could be seen on the streets, some sobbing, some laughing, some staring desolately into space as if wondering how it had come to this.

Eddie wished his former Spy High team-mates were with him. Lori or Cally or Bex. Even Jake. Even *Ben*. When Eddie had been captured in the past, the others had been there to rescue him. They wouldn't be here this time. He was on his own. If the Bad Guys got him, it'd be game over for Edward Red.

'Whitechapel 'All, guv,' announced the cabbie. Eddie paid him. ' 'Ave fun.'

He watched the cab drive off, felt the chill of the evening in his bones. On his own. With the chance to prove himself a worthy graduate of Spy High once and for all.

Inside the Whitechapel Hall chairs had been set out for the meeting. They faced a podium from which Bartholomew Knight would undoubtedly speak. Two crossed banners of the UK First Party, with the Union flag predictably prominent, were displayed behind it. Eddie was mildly surprised. The hall was already more than half full, with a good twenty minutes still to go before the advertised time for commencement. On this showing, however, he doubted that Knight's followers posed any immediate threat to national security. The average age of those present was pensionable.

He took a seat at the end of a row next to a woman who, had she been an item of clothing, would have been offloaded at a charity shop long ago. 'It's terrible, isn't it?' she informed Eddie by way of greeting.

'What is?' Eddie thought he'd better make an effort.

'It's just terrible.' The woman shook her head.

Eddie nodded his. 'Never mind,' he said understandingly. 'Mr Knight'll sort it out. UK First, right?' He'd better get used to establishing his credentials as one of Knight's supporters, particularly if he wanted to offer his services to the man after the meeting.

Then doors to the hall burst open and Eddie tensed. A clutch of perhaps a dozen thugs swaggered inside, all fists and boots and intimidation. While they were not yet enraged enough to provide pigmentary evidence, Eddie had no doubt that these were Jacks. They glared defiantly at the people already seated.

'What'choo lookin' at?' One of them thrust his head threateningly at an elderly gentleman. 'Aint'choo dead yet? Out of our way!'

As they pushed their way into one of the front rows, a side door opened and a further group entered the hall. This was led by a trio of official-seeming middle-aged and studious men in suits. Behind them followed somebody shorter who Eddie couldn't yet make out, and behind *that* person, bringing up the rear, were a quartet of bruisers who looked like bulldogs on steroids, obviously the bodyguards. But for whom? As the party made its way to the podium, the imposing figure of Bartholomew Knight was nowhere to be seen. Unless that was him crouching low behind the officials, which didn't seem quite his style. Eddie's eyes widened in surprise as the men parted. The final member of the podium party was a girl, about the same age as him, but a lot better-looking. Glossy, severely cropped black hair, clinging black dress, perfectly proportioned figure, the kind of body you had to work out for on a daily basis, and strong yet sensitive features.

There were howls and hoots of approval from the Jacks.

'Good evening, ladies and gentlemen,' Eddie saw the first official mouth. Maybe he should try switching the mic on. 'Good evening, ladies and gentlemen.' Better, but he still nearly had to shout to make himself audible above the whistles of the Jacks. 'I am afraid that . . .' Eddie strained to hear that due to unexpected illness Mr Knight would not be able to address the meeting. There were groans from some. Derision from the Jacks.

'I think it's terrible,' contributed Eddie's companion.

'But we are pleased and honoured to have with us instead, speaking to you in her father's place, the leader of our party's daughter, Ms Boudica Knight.'

She was her father's daughter, all right. The manner in which she stood – scarlet-tipped hands on hips, accepting the adulation of the audience as if it was her right and unfazed by certain improper suggestions from the Jacks – conveyed a sense of leadership that Eddie had sensed even in the hologram of Bartholomew Knight, and the concrete conviction of being right. One of the bodyguards came forward, whispered in her ear (lucky guy, Eddie thought) and gestured towards the Jacks. Boudica waved him aside regally. Yeah, Eddie thought. Like royalty. The only other Boudica he'd heard of had been a warrior queen who'd led her English tribe against the Romans. Not everything, it seemed, changed with the centuries.

'My friends,' Boudica Knight began, and she scarcely required the mic, 'supporters and fellow patriots, our nation has need of us today.'

Her speech was what Eddie imagined to be par for the course at UK First gatherings. Britain good. Europa bad. Prime Minister a traitor. Knight in shining armour.

As a Deveraux operative Eddie's only interest was in saving lives and putting Albion out of business, but if he'd been true-born British, he suspected that Boudica might have been able to sway him. Certainly most of the audience were hanging on to her every word like a drowning man with a lifeline.

The Jacks were the exception. As Boudica's speech gathered pace so did their jeering, catcalls and roars of protest. Eddie craned forward to see. It was happening. The flags were forming. As fury seized the Jacks, so their faces seemed to melt, submerge. Eddie knew what was coming next.

The podium party seemed to know it too. The officials pleaded lamely for quiet in the hall. The bodyguards flanked Boudica. Eddie wondered why there wasn't a police presence at an event with such volatile potential.

And then the storm broke.

'She's lying! Her old man's lying!' One of the Jacks raged at the audience. 'They're in on it too! They're part of the plot! Talk talk talk! It gets you nowhere and it's all lies! There's only one way to save this country. Not by votes. By action!'

The Jacks began seizing chairs and hurling them at the podium.

The audience panicked. One or two of the sprightlier men punched out at the Jacks but most surged frantically for the doors.

Eddie kept his cool. His course was clear. As was the intention of the Jacks. They were bearing down now on only one person. Boudica.

Eddie darted past the fleeing audience. He vaulted a wreckage of chairs, feeling the adrenaline pumping as he converted the chaos of the scene to a diagram in his brain, the better to plan a strategy.

It seemed the bodyguards had been earning their money under false pretences. They were bulkier and stronger than the Jacks but were grappled to the ground with scarcely a fight.

Eddie hit the podium as a grinning flag-head turned. A quick blow sent the thug sprawling. Boudica had been forced back by the onslaught, but even now her expression was proud – unafraid.

Eddie took out a second Jack, but two more were reaching for Knight's daughter, laughing and leering.

He sprang on to the podium, barrelled into them like a bowling ball into skittles, sent them crashing to the floor.

'What?' For the first time, Boudica looked startled.

'Hi.' Eddie stood with her side by side. 'My name's Eddie and I'll be your saviour from certain death tonight. If there's any particular escape plan you have in mind please ask me and I'll do everything I can to oblige.'

'Are you for real?' said Boudica.

'You can always touch me and see.'

Boudica sighed. 'I knew this evening wasn't going to go well.'

And maybe she had a point. Eddie had battled his way *in*, but could he battle his way *out* again with Boudica intact? The dozen Jacks glowering at them seemed to doubt it.

They closed in.

FOUR

Boudica glanced at Eddie. She assumed a defensive posture, one foot planted forward, arms crossed like a locked door in front of her face. 'You watch my back and I'll watch yours.'

'It'll be a pleasure,' he grinned.

With a cry that would have curdled the blood of many a martial arts master, Boudica's fist lashed out to deter the advance of the first Jack, glazing his eyes and staggering him backwards.

'Nice technique,' Eddie said.

The Jacks lunged as one.

Boudica was all yells and broad, dramatic strokes of her arms and legs – kung fu that would look good in competition. Eddie worked silently, methodically, economically – kung fu for survival. He chopped at the vital pressure points on his assailants' bodies, paralysing, temporarily disabling, and if they would have all just queued up nicely he could have got it over with quickly and they could have all gone home. But the howling Jacks would not cooperate, and he was having to fend blows off as well as strike out himself. The Jacks were stupid, they knew no tactics other than to press forward until they were either victorious or unconscious, but they were also numerous. And the stupid many were too often a match for the intelligent few.

'There's too many of them. We need an edge.'

'*You're* supposed to be doing the rescue. *I* just came to talk politics.'

Then Eddie remembered the UK First Party banners. The ones with flags where they should be, hanging from flagpoles rather than displayed on faces. It was the edge they needed.

'Grab a banner!' he shouted. 'Time for a little bit of flag-waving.'

He ducked beneath a Jack's attack, avoided a second clumsy blow and was at the back of the podium, Boudica alongside him. They seized the banners by the flag ends, swung them around. 'Okay, who wants to get swatted first?'

The Jacks, not too surprisingly, lunged forward. Eddie and Boudica slashed out with the banners, scythed low. There was the crack of wood against knee caps. The remaining Jacks faltered. Another flourish of the flagpoles, this time at chest-height, was followed by whooshes of air from suddenly emptied lungs. Eddie and Boudica came together, whirled the poles around their heads. He saw her laughing, her eyes bright.

'Shall we finish them off?' she grinned.

They didn't need to. The hall's doors were flung wide to announce the entrance of the police at last. Those Jacks still capable of independent movement opted to use it for the purpose of retreat. They didn't get far.

About as far as the cops, in fact. They seemed almost happy to be handcuffed.

The officer in charge rushed over to Boudica and Eddie full of concern. 'Ms Knight, are you all right?'

'I am,' Boudica said haughtily, 'thanks to the intervention of this young man here and *no* thanks to your men, Sergeant. It comes to something when the police force of this country is conspicuous by its absence while the daughter of one of its foremost politicians is in danger of her life. No wonder the criminal fraternity have never had it so good.'

'Ms Knight, please, I can assure you—'

'Assure my father,' Boudica dismissed. 'And then, I imagine, his lawyers.'

Cowed, the officer backed away, compensating by yelling at his minions.

'It was a good question, though,' said Eddie. '*Are* you all right?'

'Of course.' With a tinge of 'why *wouldn't* I be?' implied. 'I just won't need to use the gym when I get home. But thank you. I don't know what would have happened if you hadn't been here. I think my father needs to invest in new bodyguards.' She looked on unpityingly as the men in question staggered to their feet. 'Bring the limo to the door at once,' she snapped to one of them. 'I don't want to stay here any longer than necessary. My father needs to be informed.' She turned again to Eddie, her tone softening. 'Sorry. What did you say your name was again?'

'Eddie Nelligan,' he supplied. 'I've been a supporter of UK First for a while, but what with this conference coming up, I thought I'd like to see your father for myself. Maybe join. That's why I'm here. Figured I should get more actively involved while we've still got a country left to save.' Eddie hoped he was sounded convincing.

'But you're Irish, aren't you?'

'Part Irish, on my mother's side,' lied Eddie. 'All British, and on *your* side.'

Boudica considered, examining him thoughtfully. 'Good. That's good. You demonstrated great personal courage coming to my aid, Eddie, and you certainly know how to fight.'

'Where I grew up, you had to learn how to look after yourself. You've got some pretty good moves too.'

'Yes. I think they came with the name. And how do you look after yourself now?'

Eddie told her he was a SkyBike mechanic. 'But I'm looking for something else. You know, something more.' He felt like a fisherman dangling bait. Would Boudica bite?

'Well, Eddie Nelligan, I think I might be able to help you there.'

Seemed like she would. 'Really?' Look eager but not desperate, he cautioned himself.

'You came to see my father tonight but had to put up with me instead.'

'Believe me, Ms Knight, that hasn't been a problem.' Look *interested* but not desperate.

'Boudica,' she corrected, with perhaps a smile, 'and I'm pleased you found my speech acceptable. But even so, my father's non-appearance is at least a matter we can put right, and after I've spoken to him, he may have something to say to *you*, Eddie, about your future.'

'Well, Ms Knight, I mean, Boudica . . .' Just whatever you do, don't look *desperate*.

'Ms Knight, the wheelless is waiting.' The bodyguard back again.

'Very well. I have to go,' said Boudica. 'Talk to Critchley.' She indicated a party official who was presently receiving first aid for minor cuts and bruises, though from his agonised expression he might have been undergoing major surgery without anaesthetic. 'Let him know how I can contact you. And I *will*. Soon.' Now she did allow herself a smile, full and white. 'I'll see you later, Eddie Nelligan.'

'Believe it,' said Eddie, watching her walk away. Fishermen and bait, he thought. But *who* had hooked *whom*?

A policeman came up to him and asked for a state-ment. 'Wow,' said Eddie.

'Indeed,' said Bowler. 'It seems fortunate for you, then, Master Edward, that Mr Bartholomew Knight is not the father to a *son*.'

'You can say what you like, Bowler,' Eddie scorned, 'but I'm telling you, what happened last night is going to be really useful for us.'

It was the following day. Eddie and Bowler were seated in the holo-vision room of the apartment.

'It appears that the events at Whitechapel Hall are likely to prove of benefit to Bartholomew Knight as well,' Bowler said. 'He is already endeavouring to make politi-cal capital out of them.' He pressed a button in the arm of his chair to activate the holo-screen. All of a sudden, the news of the day was in the room with them. 'Get closer to your videvision favourites than ever before,' had been the advertising line when holo-vision had been launched. It hadn't been wrong.

Bartholomew Knight was giving a press conference from just behind Bowler's chair. He adjusted the screens' scope so that the politician shifted position to somewhere between himself and Eddie. 'Knight moving to the centre ground,' joked Eddie. 'I don't think so.'

'. . . cowardly attack on my daughter last night ought to prove once and for all,' Knight was declaring, punctuating every third word or so with an emphatic stab of the finger, '*once and for all* that the UK First Party has no truck with groups who would use violence and intimidation to achieve their ends. We reject them. We reject their methods. And those who claim otherwise are attempting to cast a slur on our good name for their own political purposes.'

'I see what you mean,' said Eddie. 'Mr Whiter Than White.'

'Today's opinion polls show a five point rise in support of UK First,' revealed Bowler. 'Nobody likes to hear of attractive young ladies threatened by thugs.'

Eddie frowned. 'You don't think Knight can have arranged for the attack *himself*, do you? I mean, he was supposed to be ill, but he looks all right now. You think he'd do that, place his own daughter in danger just to up his ratings?'

'Stranger things have happened, I understand, Master Edward,' observed Bowler, 'and more worrying things are happening now.' He clicked on to freshly released footage of the clean-up operation on the Channel Bridge. They sat among the burned-out shells of wheellesses while the emergency services went about their work. At least the bodies had been taken away. 'It seems that not content with claiming responsibility for this, Albion have today released a statement warning that they will not allow the Europa Conference to go ahead. If it does, they have threatened to take the lives of everyone who attends. Which Mr Deveraux believes provides this mission with something of a deadline, Master Edward.'

'And counting,' said Eddie grimly. 'I guess there's no question of the conference *not* taking place?'

By way of response, Bowler clicked the holo-screen's controls again. The Prime Minister spoke for him. 'The British Government never has given in to terrorism. The British Government never *will* give in to terrorism. Security will be reviewed, certainly, but I can say to you now that the Europa Conference will be held as planned. I am sure in my own mind that history will judge that we were right.' Perry Barnes held out his hands in pleading sincerity, displayed his teeth. 'And to our opponents I say this, why can't we all be friends?'

'So. Collision course,' Eddie mused. 'And it's up to me to stop the bang. Is that it, Bowler?'

'For the moment, Master Edward.' He deactivated the holo-room.

'What about forensics on those bombs?'

'Nothing, I'm afraid,' Bowler had to admit. 'The materials from which they were made and the technology involved have so far not been traced to any company or terrorist cell anywhere in the world.'

'What?' Eddie didn't believe it. 'No leads at all? You mean they just appeared out of thin air?'

The phone rang from the living-room. Eddie went to answer it.

'It seems,' pursued Bowler, 'that your incipient relationship with Boudica Knight, Master Edward, may be our best chance of progress.' He busied himself with checking the inventory of the weapons cabinet until Eddie had finished on the phone. While all calls to a Deveraux operative were monitored from Spy High anyway, it wasn't polite to eavesdrop.

'Then it looks like we're in luck,' Eddie reported several minutes later. 'That was the lady in question. Boudica wants to take me to meet her father tomorrow. If Bartholomew Knight *is* involved with the Jacks or Albion, I'll soon find out.'

A hover-limo collected Eddie from the flat and took him to a private airfield north of the capital. An aircraft was waiting for him there with UK First Party markings on the tail-plane. It was a state-of-the-art model and put the average Deveraux jet to shame. The Knights, if Eddie hadn't already gathered, were *seriously* rich.

Boudica had told him to dress casually but he'd still worn a jacket and tie. He suspected that Bartholomew Knight was the kind of man who liked certain standards to be maintained. Besides, his tie was Spy High issue and came with both a camera and a microphone woven into the fabric. Boudica herself wore a chunky sweater, boots and jodhpurs, as if she'd been interrupted during riding.

'I told you I'd call,' she said, welcoming Eddie aboard the plane.

'I'm glad you did. This is yours?'

'Do you like it? We've got another three at home.' He couldn't tell whether she was joking or not – with an inscrutable expression like that, Boudica would have made a great secret agent. 'Once we're in the air I'll show you around.'

The two of them buckled up in a fairly conventional, if very first class, cabin with seats for about thirty people. Apart from the crew, though, Eddie and Boudica had the plane all to themselves.

'We have videscreens throughout the plane,' the girl explained later during their tour, 'so the pilot can talk to us directly or to my dad from either his study or the meeting-room. We have a kitchen, a dining area, a relaxation area where we can watch videvision or play interactive games . . .' Boudica led Eddie through each.

'Do you have a sit down open-mouthed with astonishment area?'

'Very funny, Eddie. A little boys' room. A little girls' room.'

'You have both?'

'Of course. It's only civilised.'

'And what's this? Some kind of futuristic shower?' Eddie poked his head into a compartment lined with flickering electronic instrumentation and featuring at its centre a rounded, slightly raised dais immediately beneath a similarly circular bulge of lights set into the roof.

'Tractor beam compartment,' Boudica supplied. 'When it's operational the floor opens up and we can transfer to or from the ground without the plane having to land. We also have a hover function to keep the aircraft steady while we do it, a bit like a helicopter. You just stand on the dais there and I activate this control here. Want to give it a go?'

'You trying to get rid of me or something?'

'Why would I want to do that?' Boudica grinned. 'But it'll take about an hour to get to Little England, so we need to find something to do.'

Eddie gulped. 'Little *what*?'

'You'll see.' Her arms snaked around Eddie's neck. The camera in his tie was being treated to an *extreme* close-up of Boudica Knight; her heartbeat boomed in the microphone. So did Eddie's, which seemed to be getting faster.

Some time later Eddie caught his first glimpse of Little England. They were flying over an estate of anachronisms. As far as the eye could see were buildings, statues, towers and monuments from every age of British history – clustered together in apparently random groups, like guests at a party, a highly select party. He saw Buckingham Palace, the Tower of London, Nelson's Column, St. Paul's Cathedral. All rubbing stone shoulders one with the other. And not miniatures, either, not reconstructions in modern materials. The original structures. The original landmarks. Removed from the sites of their birth and collected together here.

'What is this?' Eddie said, bemused. 'Some kind of historical theme park?'

'Hardly.' Boudica didn't seem amused. It seemed to Eddie that her mood was becoming more intense the closer they came to landing. 'Little England is my father's life's work. In an age obsessed with the present, my father believes in the past.' They swooped past the peaks of Tower Bridge, the Thames that it once had straddled swapped now for a babbling brook, as if the Bridge had entered a genteel retirement. 'In a time when we're taught to be ashamed of our history, to turn our backs on our heritage and embrace a new world, my father has refused. Look around you, Eddie. Every construction here has been condemned over the years as unnecessary, obsolete, a poor advertisement for modern Britain. Every one was either going to be bulldozed or allowed to quietly decay, to be forgotten. My father wasn't having that. My father brought them here. And one day, he'll return them to their rightful places. Because all this is what Britain means, Eddie. All this is what Britain *is*.'

A bunch of empty old buildings, Eddie thought, but he was quick enough to say: 'It's something else, Boudica.'

He noticed that not every structure in Little England was antique. There were groups of modern buildings, offices, maybe, at a safe distance from the relics, and a monorail that nosed above the spires and turrets, reached by glass elevators ascending to platforms atop pillars of steel.

'My father's dream,' Boudica said distantly, 'to restore this country to the greatness it deserves. It's a dream I share, Eddie. I hope you do, too.'

'Absolutely,' said Eddie.

'My father is an exceptional man, a visionary,' she gestured expansively. 'That's one reason why I'd do anything for him, why I love him so much.'

'I can see that,' said Eddie, biting his lip, hoping that Knight was on the level. Because if he *wasn't*, if he *did* have anything to do with Albion and terrorism, then Eddie didn't want to be around when Boudica found out.

Bartholomew Knight dominated real life just as he did the videvision screen. He came forward at the landing strip to greet his daughter and Eddie with the moral and emotional force of a hurricane battering a coastline.

'So you're Eddie Nelligan. It's a pleasure to meet you. Boudica tells me you were something of a life-saver at the meeting the other night.'

'I only did what any right-minded patriot would do,' Eddie said modestly.

Bartholomew Knight approved. 'A pity that right-minded patriots are in short supply these days, while our enemies are all around us. But come, let me show you the sights. Boudica?'

'Do you think I'm gonna leave him all to you, Dad?'

'Tower!' snapped Knight. 'Ben!'

Two bodyguards joined them. Eddie reckoned they must have been over seven feet tall and nearly as wide. They'd have made Goliath look like David.

'Dad's personal bodyguards,' grinned Boudica. 'We call them Big Ben and the Tower of London.'

'You don't say.' The bodyguards' mouths wrinkled in what might have been a welcome. Eddie beamed back. Once more he begged for Bartholomew Knight's innocence. The prospect of having to take on Big Ben and the Tower was not an inviting one.

Knight led them to an elevator and then aboard the monorail. The latter's single cabin was more like a plusher version of the interior of a cable car than the carriage of a train. It was fully automated and voice activated, responding to Knight's commands like a pet dog.

Boudica's father beckoned for Eddie to stand with him. 'My daughter tells me you wish to join our party, to assist us in our work, our crusade.'

'Absolutely, sir,' said Eddie. 'I've always been a big fan of Richard the Lionheart.'

Knight smiled thinly. 'Well, as I implied earlier, we can always use another young person of character and intelligence in our organisation, and you've certainly made a strong impression on my daughter, Eddie.' He turned to the window as the monorail continued its unhurried journey. 'Tell me, when you look outside, what do you see?'

'It's York Minster, isn't it?' said Eddie, grateful for the research Bowler had made him do.

'In a sense, I suppose it is. Literally,' acknowledged Bartholomew Knight. 'But in another sense, a more profound and important sense, it is a thousand years of history. We have to look to our past to forge our future, Eddie. You'll have to understand that if you want to join our *true* mission. Barnes and Glover's cowardly government – Barnes and Glover! They sound like a gentleman's outfitters, do they not? – their *treacherous* government and its obsession with Europa, the Treaty Conference itself, these are only the latest threats to this nation's sovereignty and heritage. Our enemies surround us, like the seas that beat on our island shores. I have declared myself the protector of our heritage, and I will do anything and everything within my power to defend this land from those who would destroy it.'

Eddie stole a glance at Knight's eyes. They were black

coals of intensity. The leader of the UK First Party was driven, obsessed, a fanatic. His words and body language suggested text book megalomania and borderline paranoid psychosis. Spy High students would be doing a case study of Bartholomew Knight one day, of that Eddie now had no doubt. He was beginning to believe he'd come to the right place for Albion. He decided to drop a few hints.

'If only the conference could be stopped,' he suggested, 'like Albion—'

'Albion are terrorists and murderers.' Knight regarded Eddie closely. 'I have publically repudiated their methods many times.'

'Of course, Mr Knight, sir. I'm sorry, sir.' Eddie did a good abject apology. Over the years, he'd had a lot of practice. 'I didn't mean to—'

'You have sympathy with them, do you?'

'No, sir. Of course not.' And then, a master stroke. 'Not if *you* don't . . .'

Knight was duly flattered. 'Our little excursion is almost over,' he noted as the monorail eased alongside a platform, 'and I have business to attend to. But we will talk again, young man. I think I can find an opening for you that will suit your temperament. For now, though, I'll leave you in the capable hands of my daughter.'

She hugged him excitedly as they made their way towards one of the new buildings in Little England. 'He *liked* you. Dad liked you, Eddie. I could tell,' she chirped. 'But then a lot of people do.'

Would *you*, though? he wondered silently. If you knew why I really wanted to get close to your father?

'Hey, cheer up,' laughed Boudica. 'I know my dad can

be a little overpowering when you meet him for the first time, but you came through, didn't you? Let's see those pearly whites.'

Eddie smiled. The spy with a smile.

'That's better. Now let's get something to eat before we fly you back to London. There's a rec room here for the people Dad employs to maintain this place.'

She led him inside. Groups of Knight's employees were sitting or standing around, snacking, drinking, talking, shooting pool.

Eddie froze.

'Eddie? Is something wrong?'

His eyes were fixed on a guy with a shaven head and a sneer like a scar. A guy whose career interests had never included the careful restoration of venerable old buildings as far as Eddie knew. More like the absolute demolition of shiny new ones.

'Eddie? What is it?'

He hadn't seen him since the Anarchy Academy, but two years hadn't changed him. They hadn't changed Eddie that much either.

If he could recognise Frankie Garvey, Frankie Garvey would certainly recognise him.

Spy with a smile? More like spy in a sweat.

Garvey got up and came towards them.

FIVE

He hadn't noticed them yet, though, was talking to somebody else.

Eddie knew he couldn't run out the door or throw a blanket over his head, even if one was available. He turned to the quizzical Boudica. There was only one way to hide his face within the next two seconds.

He swept her up in his arms, pressed his lips against hers and snogged for all he was worth. It didn't have to be challenging Bella's record (not that he would have minded), just long enough for Frankie Garvey and friend to pass by harmlessly.

There were a few cheers from those nearby. He thought he heard Garvey laugh mere inches behind him and squinted out of the corner of his eye until he was certain the one-time trainee terrorist had left the room. Only then did he let Boudica go, half-expecting a slap. Fortunately for his cheek, it didn't come.

'What was that all about?' she demanded, without hostility.

'Oh. Just.' *Fabricate*, Eddie. 'Being here. Meeting

your father at last. Getting my chance with UK First.
Being with you.'

'Well,' Boudica grinned, 'maybe I should bring you
here more often, only I think I've got a better idea.'

'You have?' He was feeling more secure again. 'I'm
always open to better ideas.'

'There's going to be a party at our place next Saturday.
A big one. Probably hundreds of guests. Feel like
making it hundreds and one?'

'By "your place" do you mean the mansion your dad
uses as a backdrop for his party political videcasts?'

'I know it's not much,' said Boudica, 'but we like to
think of it as home. At least it's got guest-rooms. You
could stay the night.'

'And you really want me to come?' Boudica nodded.
'Then I'll be there.'

'Excellent. But Eddie, there's one thing I ought to tell
you about this party . . .'

Several days later and the subject was still on Eddie's mind
as he and Bowler conversed in the flat's Weapons Room. 'I
mean, I know it's a gift for us,' he was saying. 'The invita-
tion gets me into Knight's private residence. I socialise a
bit, laugh at people's jokes, have a few drinks . . .'

'Of a non-alcoholic variety, Master Edward,'
reminded Bowler sagely. 'Deveraux agents do not drink
on missions.'

'As if.' Eddie feigned shock. 'And then I just kind of
slip away and look for something incriminating.
Shouldn't be too hard to find, either. If Knight employs
sleazebags like Frankie Garvey, chances are he *is* our
man after all.'

'Indeed,' acknowledged Bowler. 'In fact, Mr Garvey was not the only known terrorist that your tie camera allowed us to identify. We have already increased our surveillance of Little England.' He paused, regarded Eddie thoughtfully. 'Might one observe, however, Master Edward, that even given the success of your operation thus far, you do not appear especially happy.'

'It's Boudica,' Eddie admitted. 'When we do have to take her father down, what's that going to do to her? She worships him. She doesn't deserve it. I mean, it's not her fault her dad's a lunatic, is it? But . . .' He was suddenly aware of Bowler's scrutiny and stopped. Reddened. 'Sorry. I was getting carried away, wasn't I?'

'Might one remind you, Master Edward,' said Bowler, not unkindly, 'that it is never wise for an agent to become personally or emotionally involved in a mission, whatever the provocation or – how can one put it? – encouragement. One must remain cool and clinical in the field at all times. Reserved.'

'Like you, Bowler?' Eddie said, and he wasn't sure whether he intended to be critical or not.

Bowler's chiselled and impeccably presented visage remained impassive in any case. 'Sleepshot, Master Edward,' he said. 'You'll be wearing sleepshot wrist-bands on Saturday, of course. This pair here, in fact.' He pressed a stud in the wall and panels slid silently open like well-oiled wardrobe doors. What was displayed behind them, however, was not clothing. Bowler ignored the shock blasters, the stasis rifles and the flash grenades in boxes, like eggs, and retrieved a square, apparently perspex container within which the sleepshot wrist-bands could be seen. He placed the container on a stand that had risen from the floor.

'Still boxed up?' said Eddie. 'What, haven't got round to unpacking the latest shipment from Deveraux yet, Bowler?'

The older man did not rise to his charge's teasing. 'These wrist-bands are the first of a new design, Master Edward,' he explained. 'They may look the same as ever, but they now contain a feature that might prove useful were you to be unfortunately parted from them.'

'What? You mean if I get caught? Spy High sure has a lot of faith in me,' Eddie grumbled.

'This new model is now standard issue for all field operatives, Master Edward,' said Bowler, 'including, it seems, those with a propensity for insecurity.'

'Okay. Point taken.' Eddie was abashed. 'So what do they do?'

'They can be voice-activated,' Bowler informed. 'Each band has been programmed to recognise its owner's voice. The technicians used the vocal records that remain on every agent's file at Deveraux to personalise them.'

'But that means they can hear me now, surely? Why aren't they activating?'

'Because it would not be sensible for sleepshot to be fired every time you speak, Master Edward,' Bowler pointed out, 'though that *would* perhaps be of benefit by encouraging you to question whether what you want to say is truly worth saying.'

'Yeah, good one. Maybe I could mime my way through a mission.'

'No, to activate the sleepshot, Master Edward, you need to whistle.'

Eddie whistled.

It was as well Bowler had kept the wrist-bands in their container. The perspex material was immediately studded with sleepshot shells, enough to incapacitate half a room of bad guys.

'I guess that works,' said Eddie.

'And now, the party, Master Edward,' continued Bowler. 'The costume theme is perfect.'

'Yeah. British heroes.' Eddie smiled thinly. 'I reckon Knight'll end up going as himself.'

'But you, Master Edward,' Bowler announced, 'will be attending as Admiral Nelson, which will allow us to equip you with one or two other little trinkets. For example . . .'

Admiral Horatio Nelson, hero of the Battle of Trafalgar, 1805. He won the battle but lost his life. Eddie hoped that wasn't a pointer for how his own mission might go. And Bowler might have been happy with his choice of famous figure, but Eddie felt that Shakespeare or Churchill or Alfred the Great might have been easier to carry off in some ways. At least their bodies were pretty much complete. During his eventful naval career, Nelson had lost both his right arm and his right eye. It kind of meant that if Garvey was at the party and leaping at him from the right, Eddie was going to be at something of a disadvantage. The eye-patch and the right sleeve of his uniform which was sewn to the tunic were not negotiable.

Boudica had sent a hover-limo for him which was just as well. Even Eddie might have struggled to fly a SkyBike one-handed. They entered the grounds of

Bartholomew Knight's mansion as the sun set. The estate made the grounds at Spy High look like an allotment: endless woodland that gradually rose to rim the horizon like a bowl, at the centre of which stood the house. It was lit up by spotlights placed at every conceivable angle, highlighting historical figures on the lawns and by the marquees. Eddie's hover-limo lowered itself in the parking area, gently, so as not to inconvenience the gravel.

'You want a hand there, Admiral?' said the chauffeur. 'Looks like one of yours is missing.'

'Yeah. The one I tip with,' Eddie retorted. 'Don't give up the day job.'

Nelson joined the throng of his fellow notables, all of them looking a lot happier than when they'd last walked the earth. The Duke of Wellington, Lord Cardigan and Field-Marshall Montgomery were perhaps discussing past campaigns. Henry VIII, an oddly bespectacled Queen Victoria and an indeterminate number of Edwards and Georges were no doubt commenting on the trials and tribulations of king- and queenship. Nearby and extending the royal theme, Charles I and Anne Boleyn seemed to be comparing their necks, both blemishless of the executioner's axe. Margaret Thatcher and Tony Blair were holding hands and canoodling in a corner, and several William Shakespeares seemed to be debating which of them had *really* been responsible for 'King Lear' and 'Hamlet' over champagne and canapes.

'Hi.' Eddie started as a hand grabbed his shoulder. Luckily it was Boudica and not Frankie Garvey, particularly as a kiss as well as a hug was involved.

'Hi yourself.'

'You're looking very smart.' Boudica admired the bemedalled blue tunic Eddie was wearing, the spotless, stiff-collared shirt beneath, even the broad Admiral's hat that perched at a severe angle on his head like a ship about to sink. 'I never thought I could be attracted to someone called Horatio, but it seems there's a first time for everything. Maybe I should have come as Lady Hamilton.'

'I guess there's no prize for guessing who you *have* come as?' laughed Eddie. The crown. The cloak. The tasteful daubs of woad on the cheeks. 'Queen Boudica of the Iceni, I presume. Didn't notice your chariot parked anywhere.'

'You think it's a little obvious?' Boudica looked down at her costume.

'Absolutely. I think you should remove it at once.'

'Oh, yeah,' Boudica smiled. 'So you can watch.'

'Don't worry about me,' Eddie quipped 'I'm 'armless. And besides, as the song kind of says, I only have eye for you.'

Boudica groaned. 'Whoever writes your material, Eddie, fire him.' She lifted his eye-patch up over his forehead. 'That's better. Now you can see me in stereo. Come on.'

'We're going inside?' Eddie looked up at the prim, slightly reproving Georgian exterior of the mansion, wondering what secrets he might divine within later.

'No. All the fogeys are in there,' Boudica disapproved. 'Sitting in armchairs dressed as old soldiers even *I* haven't heard of.'

'The fogeys or the armchairs?'

'They're all drinking port and droning on about the

good old days. Thatcherism and all that stuff. I mean, I support my dad and UK First, you know that, but there's a time and a place, don't you think? We'll try the marquees. There's a different band in each one. You can show me whether your dancing's as good as your fighting, Admiral.'

'Sadly, my dancing's all at sea,' Eddie said. 'Is your dad around, Boudica?'

'Somewhere.' Boudica seemed faintly upset by the question. 'Why? You'd sooner dance with him than me?'

'Obviously not. No. Nothing like that.' With his one free arm Eddie steered her around the side of the nearest marquee, into one of the few scraps of shadow that had survived the spotlights. They could hear the music from within, sounds of laughter and merriment.

'So? Dad knows I like you. You haven't got to watch out for him or anything.'

'It's not that. It's just . . . your dad.' Bowler's words reverberated in Eddie's brain like a cruel echo that just happened to be true. Mission. Emotional involvement. Not a relationship that had a future. But how could he *not* warn her? 'Can I ask you a question? I know we've not known each other long but, well, it's a serious question.'

'You're not about to propose are you?' Boudica grinned.

'It's more a kind of what if.' Eddie didn't smile back. 'About your dad. Look, I know he strongly believes in his cause. I know *you* do, Boudica. I do, too.'

'So?' She regarded him strangely, as though uncertain of him for the first time.

'So, what if he was ever tempted to go, you know, too far? To think in terms of violent protest, armed struggle. I mean, what if he ever thought about getting involved with something like Albion, that could endanger you?'

Boudica stared at him blankly for a moment, as if his words were having to be translated for her. Then she burst into laughter. 'Is that it? Is that all? Your serious question?' She threw her arms around his neck and kissed him. 'It'll never happen, you idiot. Dad's against violence. He's said so hundreds of times.'

'Yeah, but Boudica . . .'

She stopped his lips with her fingers. 'He always means what he says. And so do I. Don't worry. Dad knows what he's doing, and he'd never do anything to harm me. It's not going to happen. But it's sweet of you to be so concerned, Eddie.'

'Well,' Eddie backtracked, sensing he was unlikely to make progress tonight, 'just being patriotic.'

What had he hoped to achieve anyway, talking to Boudica like that? Dropping dumb hints. How could he make her suspicious of the father she'd hero-worshipped for every minute of her eighteen years? *'Boudica, your beloved father is a terrorist. He employs terrorists and may well be the brains behind Albion. I know because I'm not Admiral Nelson. I'm not even Eddie Nelligan, SkyBike mechanic. I'm actually a secret agent trained at Spy High and employed by the Deveraux organisation to keep the world safe for tomorrow.'* A spiel like that *might* work, but it would certainly compromise the integrity of his mission And there was still so much to do.

Like, for example, find some *evidence*. Eddie temporarily

evaded Boudica with a visit to the men's room. She'd whipped the hat from his head as a kind of hostage to guarantee his return.

It was lucky she hadn't stolen his eye-patch too because now, as he hastened into the mansion, adjusting it over his right eye, its true value became apparent. The patch did not *impede* Eddie's vision, it *enhanced* it. A web of sensors and circuitry hidden beneath the mock leather material meant he could now see through walls, floors and ceilings. The Optical Environment Assimilator's instrumentation was attuned to detect abnormally large sources of electrical power as well. Would-be world conquerors tended not to be energy efficient.

And it didn't look like Bartholomew Knight was going to be any different in that respect, even if the scope of his ambitions did seem limited to one country rather than all of them. The OEA was alerting Eddie to a significant energy source not far ahead of him. The mansion seemed to have negligible internal security – the OEA was aware of no spy cameras or tripbeams or anything like that – but then, Knight had invited only friends and supporters to his house. He wasn't expecting any of his guests to be prowling the innermost corridors of his mansion, as Eddie was now, reaching what appeared to be a blank stone wall and not accepting it as such. And Knight probably wasn't anticipating any of his invitees to come equipped with a device that could clearly identify the door camouflaged in the stone and the high-tech control centre beyond. He certainly wouldn't have been prepared for anybody to whom he'd extended his hospitality to abuse that trust by breaking through. To do so would not be the English way.

But it was the Spy High way.

Eddie prepared himself, tearing the right sleeve away from his costume. The age of miracles was clearly not yet past: Nelson had his strong right arm back again. He needed it.

Next Eddie detached one of the medals, pointing it at where his OEA was telling him the invisible entrance's locking mechanism was to be found. He turned the rim of the medal clockwise. It fired a laser bolt, deactivating the lock and opening the door. So far so good, Eddie thought, stepping through. The door closed behind him. The OEA having served its purpose, he pulled it off and thrust it into his pocket.

The control centre was modest by the standards he was used to – the usual banks of computers, screens and other nefarious instrumentation only on a smaller scale. But there was something unusual: the doorway was guarded on the inside by a pair of suits of armour, full-size, on plinths, one holding a sword, the other an axe, neither living nor posing a threat. A little bit of medieval tradition, Eddie guessed. Maybe Knight should have got up to date and posted a guard instead. As it was, there was nothing to stop intruders from simply sitting themselves down at the nearest available computer and hacking their way into all his little secrets.

The only hacking that came naturally to Eddie was when he had a cough, he was no instinctive cyber-whizz, but he'd learned his lessons well at Spy High. It didn't take him long to bypass Knight's security protocols. 'Albion,' he whispered. 'Where are you?'

There was no sign of Albion. But something else

caught his eye. Filename: Pendragon Project. Wasn't Pendragon King Arthur's family name? That sounded very Bartholomew Knight. Spy High agents were trained to follow their instincts, even if doing so temporarily diverted them from the initial focus of operations. Eddie entered the Pendragon Project file.

Spy High agents were also trained to expect danger, at all times and from the unlikeliest sources. For example, a suit of armour that came alive and tried to behead you with an axe.

The swish through the air gave it away. Eddie was diving and rolling as the axe's deadly arc severed the space where seconds ago his neck would have been.

'If you wanted to use the computer, you could have just asked,' he complained, assuming a crouched defensive posture.

Both suits were moving towards him, their weapons raised.

Eddie fired sleepshot. The shells drilled into his attackers' breast-plates to no effect. 'Okay, so you're animates. That's cool. I just won't expect conversation.'

The axe guillotined towards him. Eddie leaped. The sword flashed out and almost intercepted him. But Eddie was too quick. It was the almost that kept you alive.

He grabbed for a medal again. The axe-wielder had driven his weapon into the floor, was tugging it out. A sitting duck. Eddie fired. Couldn't miss. The deactivator beam made the armoured animate crackle and jerk, its final movements before its electronic joints seized up and it froze into uselessness.

'Sorry,' said Eddie, 'but you axed for that.'

Its companion, though, was still active. Eddie turned to face it. Its visor lifted automatically. Light glittered like a sadist's smile behind it – a pulse-charge.

It fired and Eddie fired at the same time. The difference was, Eddie fired while in motion but the animate remained stationary. Eddie evaded the ray aimed at him. The animate did not.

'Thanks for the work-out, guys. Better luck next time.'

Time. How much did he have left? Somehow, maybe simply by entering the room, he'd activated the animate guards. What if his presence had also alerted Knight's human minions? They could be hurtling through the corridors towards him even now. He'd better cut his losses and leave. The Pendragon Project would have to wait.

The door obediently opened for him. Or rather, not for him.

Big Ben and the Tower of London bulged into the control centre.

'What do you guys eat for *breakfast*?' Eddie gaped disbelievingly. Surely they'd grown since he'd seen them at Little England. They were at least seven feet tall. Their fists like boulders with veins. The shock blasters they carried were lost in them.

'Eat?' grinned Ben. 'We eat little squirts like you. We like the way your bones crunch, don't we, Tower?'

'Yeah, well you know what they say,' said Eddie, backing away as the giants advanced, 'the bigger they are, the harder they fall. So this is gonna hurt.'

Shock blasts and sleepshot exploded simultaneously. Eddie sought cover behind a console. Tower and Ben's fire sparked off the metal, dazzling his sight. They moved with astonishing speed for such big men, almost as if their motor centres had been artificially accelerated. He wasn't hitting them either. It was a stand-off. And sooner or later in a stand-off, two would almost always get the better of one.

But what if Eddie could raise some reinforcements?

It was lucky Nelson had been so highly decorated. He reached for the medal again. Clockwise for deactivation. Anti-clockwise for *re*activation. Eddie fired at the lifeless animates. It was better than a defibrillator. Unsteady on their metal legs, the animates were nevertheless once more awake. And looking for a fight.

As Eddie had seen, Big Ben and the Tower of London were closer to the suits of armour than he was. As he'd *hoped*, the animates' present programming did not permit them to differentiate between intruders who worked for Bartholomew Knight and intruders who did not. They took the first available foe.

Three to two. Much healthier.

But Eddie's advantage maybe wouldn't last for ever. Ben was staggering the sword-wielder with a sequence of shock blasts, buckling its breast-plate. Tower was wrestling with the axe-man like he was going to yank its artificial arm out of its electronic socket. Eddie wouldn't put it past him.

Time to go.

He darted out between the battles on either side. One of the giants, Eddie couldn't see who, tried to pick him off before he reached the door. Failed, though he could feel the heat of the shock blast as it scorched the wall to his left. He was through the door, not slackening his pace. He reckoned he'd pretty much outstayed his welcome.

Eddie's cover was blown. Tower and Ben had seen him at Little England. When they'd finished with the animates, they'd report the fact to Bartholomew Knight and then they'd no doubt try again to finish *him*. Eddie didn't like to be the first one to leave a party, but in this case he'd make an exception.

He careered through corridors. Somebody was in his way. Not an animate or one of Knight's henchmen. More impassable than either of those. Boudica. She was still holding his hat.

'Eddie, I was coming to find . . . what *happened*?'

He could ignore her, run past her, get out while the getting was good. Or he could tell her the truth, delay his escape for crucial minutes. What would an agent emotionally uninvolved with the mission do? Who cared? That wasn't Eddie.

'We've got to talk. Where can we go?'

'Can't we talk here? Eddie, I don't —'

'No. It has to be somewhere that's not public.'

'Okay. Okay.' His urgency seemed to baffle her. 'We can go to my room if you like.'

'Your room's good.' He glanced behind him. There were no signs of pursuit as yet. 'Quickly.'

Boudica led him there. A suite of rooms rather than just the one, but Eddie wasn't interested in accommodation just now. He crossed to a window and looked outside. The party was still in full swing. He had a chance, then.

'Now do you mind telling me what this sudden secrecy thing's all about? I've still got your hat here.'

'I don't care about the stupid hat.' Eddie knocked it to the floor as it was offered. 'I care about you, Boudica, and what I've got to say . . . I'm really sorry. I really wish I didn't have to tell you, but you need to know. I'm not who you think I am.'

'You're not gay, are you?'

'Boudica, I'm serious. I tried to warn you earlier. I'm a spy. A secret agent. I'm investigating your father.'

'What?' Boudica gave a short, still-born laugh. 'What do you mean?'

'That's what I've been doing this evening. I've been attacked, nearly killed. Boudica, who knows what your father's into, but it's bad. I think he's behind Albion. He may even have been responsible for the assault on the Channel Bridge. Boudica?'

Her head had dropped. Her shoulders were hunched forward. She sighed. 'I don't believe it. I just don't believe it.'

'You've got to believe it. I can fire sleepshot if you like, prove I'm what I say I am, prove I'm telling you the truth. You have to *listen* to me, Boudica.'

'I am listening to you, Eddie. That's the problem.' She drifted across the room to a cabinet standing against the wall, opened it.

Eddie pursued her. 'The Jacks who attacked you at the meeting, I think your dad even put them up to it. You're not safe.'

'Ah,' said Boudica, 'you're wrong there on both counts, Eddie. The Jacks disrupting the meeting, threatening me, a helpless girl, and earning the party lots of good publicity . . .'

Alarm bells rang too late in Eddie's mind.

'That was all *my* idea.' Boudica turned. The shock blaster she held was pressed against his chest, the barrel as cold as her eyes. 'And as for personal safety, I think it's *you* who needs to worry about that. Don't you?'

SIX

They'd taken his tunic and his sleepshot and he'd let them. They'd shoved him into a surprisingly modern elevator that had taken them below the mansion to a guard-room, to a cell, and he hadn't protested. He hadn't even put up token resistance when they'd sealed him inside. Why should he? His present situation was entirely his own fault. He'd been stupid, blind, and worse – amateurish. He was supposed to be espionage literate. He should have been able to read the signs. Why hadn't it even occurred to him that Boudica's adulatory loyalty to her father might extend to complicity in his crimes? Because she had a pretty face, that was why. Because she looked good in her costume. Whatever the final fate of Edward Red, and things didn't seem hopeful from here, he'd at least have the satisfaction of knowing that the students would be learning about him at Spy High for many years to come – as the definitive example of why *not* to let feelings interfere with field operations.

Eddie had kind of hoped for a more positive immortality than that.

He stepped back from the energy beams that barred the cell with quick-frying voltages, turned to settle dismayed eyes on its interior. Received something of a surprise.

He wasn't alone. There was only one bed, the usual wooden frame and blanket, and somebody had already claimed it, was sitting on it with her legs drawn up under her chin and the blanket around her shoulders. *Her*. A girl.

She was sixteen, maybe seventeen, dressed in a kind of shapeless, colourless one-piece, as if her tailor had been given incorrect measurements and didn't care anyway. Her hair was even redder than Eddie's, and long, and not noticeably clean. She was sprinkled with freckles and her green eyes seemed lost, fixed on sights that could not be shared. Her lips moved, like she was talking to someone, but no sound came out and no one replied. She seemed not to have noticed Eddie immediately, either.

'Sorry. Didn't see you there. If they grant me a last request I'd better fix an appointment with an optician.'

The girl still seemed unaware of Eddie's presence, not reacting in the slightest.

'So,' he tried again, 'what's a nice girl like you doing in a cell like this?'

She wasn't saying.

Eddie frowned. Who was she? Why was she here? What had Knight done to her? There was something about her, she seemed so lonely and helpless. Eddie felt indignation rise up within him, an anger at Bartholomew Knight that he should keep a girl who was obviously mentally challenged in some way here in a cell. And he was glad of his anger. It meant he was recovering from his shock over Boudica. It meant he was becoming a functioning secret agent again. It meant he wasn't dead yet.

First, though, the girl. 'My name's Eddie,' he said, approaching her cautiously. She didn't meet his gaze, chose to stare down at the floor. He knelt in front of her. 'Do you have a name?'

And suddenly she was looking directly at him. 'Everyone has a name. Every*thing* has a name. It's how we organise the world.'

'Guess it is. Guess it is.' Progress. She talked.

'Guess? Don't you know?' And she made smart comments, even if Eddie suspected she didn't realise it. 'You wouldn't make much of a scientist.'

'Probably not. But my name's Eddie. And you are . . .?'

'I'm Rose. The prettiest rose in England, my father says, but I rather suspect he's biased. A scientist should always retain his objectivity.'

'So I've heard,' Eddie said, regarding the girl called Rose more curiously than ever. She was a baffling mixture of old and young, her language evidently quite advanced but her general manner immature, as if she'd been starved of opportunities to socialise with people of her own age. 'Your father's a scientist, then, is he?'

'A very great scientist,' she perked up. 'He's made amazing advances in many fields, particularly bio-technology.'

'What's his name? Maybe I've heard of him.' Maybe he was working for Knight – but if so, why was his daughter so plainly a prisoner?

Rose shook her head emphatically. 'You won't have heard of him. Nobody outside the project *can* have heard of him.'

'Project?' The file on Knight's computer system. 'You mean the Pendragon Project?'

Rose's face lit up with delight. 'You know of us. Then you can help us. You must know how important my father's work is.' She reached out, clutched Eddie's arm. Her fingers were slender but strong. 'I can't let them keep me here any longer, Eddie. My father needs me. You've got to help me escape, help me get back to the project. You'll do that, won't you? I have to see my father.'

'I'm afraid that won't be possible just yet, little Rose.'

The girl shrank back and Eddie wheeled, snapped into combat readiness. On the other side of the energy beams, they had company.

'Your father has other priorities that concern him at the moment,' added Bartholomew Knight. 'And so, Eddie or whatever your real name might be, how are you settling in?'

'Well if you call that bucket over there the en suite, Knight, think I might put in a complaint. And what's this, anyway?' Eddie indicated the man's companions. 'A family outing?'

Boudica stood alongside her father. He tried not to look directly at her, half-afraid of what he might see in her eyes. Contempt, maybe. Loathing. Hatred. Nothing good. The emotional frost of fanaticism. And she'd been such a good kisser, too.

Both she and Knight wore conventional, if flamboyant, clothing again. 'No more costumes?' Eddie said. 'So I take it the party's over.'

'It is for you, Neilson.' Ah, that voice, after all these months, the embittered tones of someone for whom his place in life was never going to be sufficient. 'Or Nelligan. Or whatever it is you're calling yourself now.' Frankie Garvey muscled his way to the front of the grinning lackeys Knight had brought with him. 'Remember me?'

'Sure I do, Frankie.' Keep it light, confident. 'With a face that ugly, how could I forget? Still keeping choice company, I see.'

The sneer spread, like rabies. 'Mr Knight is a man of vision, Eddie, a man of conviction. And he's got the strength to make things happen. I remember telling you about the strong and the weak before, and here's proof. Me on the winning side, you in a cell like the loser you always were. But why should I be surprised, Eddie? I'd have put you out of your misery before if it hadn't been for that blond guy saving your skin.'

'Well if you want to give it another try, you know where to find me.'

'Enough,' snapped Bartholomew Knight. 'Your individual rivalry is of no interest to me. Garvey, keep your mind on what you're here for. Nelligan, back against the wall, if you please, and hands on your head.'

'You didn't say Simon Says,' noted Eddie. Half a dozen shock blasters pointed at him through the energy beams. 'That'll do nicely.' He backed against the wall and put his hands on his head. There was no way he could overcome the number of men Knight had mustered, not here and now. He'd have to bide his time.

Knight's voice softened, from a lion to a snake. 'Rose, my dear, we'd like you to come with us. We have some new accommodation for you just along here where you can be alone. Where you won't be subjected to any corrupting influences.'

'Corrupting . . .? You don't mean me, do you?' Eddie was offended. 'We've only just met. I'm not a corrupting influence, am I, Boudica?'

Boudica sniffed. 'More a minor annoyance, Eddie.'

'Switch off the beams,' ordered Knight, 'and Nelligan, if you even blink before they go on again they won't *need* to go on again. Do you understand me?'

'Sure. But if I nod you'll kill me, right?'

The cell's energy beams were deactivated. Blasters still trained on Eddie, several lackeys entered, laid their hands on Rose. 'Gently, gently,' admonished Knight. 'She's too precious to harm.'

'Don't touch me.' Rose twisted in her captors' grasp. 'Let *go* of me.'

Knight's men did not comply. They dragged Rose out of sight, out of hearing. The power was restored to the cell.

'Can I move now?' Eddie asked.

'If you wish.'

'So who's the girl? I'd figured you were low-life, Knight, but locking up a girl who's clearly one flag short of a country is kind of *subterranean*-life, if you don't mind me saying.'

'Not at all, Nelligan,' said Knight generously. 'By all means, make full use of your vocal chords. While you still have them. But if you think I'm going to tell you about Rose, then you are sadly mistaken. My business is my own, and I do not approve of anyone attempting to pry into it without my consent.'

'Guess I'm off your Christmas card list, then.'

'Boudica told me of your claim to be a spy. Your equipment has confirmed it, and Garvey supplied certain details about your past.' Knight drew himself up more powerfully and dramatically than ever, like a movie star ready for the big close up. 'I don't know what organisation you work for and I don't care. Let it do its worst. Let it send what agents it can. Bartholomew Knight will not be thwarted. I will save this country from those who would betray it. I will make Britain truly great again.'

'And if innocent people die along the way,' interjected Eddie, 'well, you can't make an omelette without breaking a few eggs, right?'

'Any noble cause incurs casualties, Nelligan,' said Knight. 'They are unfortunate but inevitable if the greater good is to prevail. What are the lives of individuals compared to the glorious immortality of our nation?'

'So you and Albion are all pals together, right, Bart?'

'I *am* Albion,' declared Knight. '*That* I am proud for you to know. Our enemies may try to dismiss us as terrorists, but in time, after our victory, we will be seen with clearer eyes as the crusaders we truly are, risking our lives in the cause of our country's freedom.'

'Yeah, yeah,' Eddie scoffed. 'Hey, Boudica, is it time for your Dad's medication yet?'

But Boudica was enthralled by her father's speech. Eddie'd have better luck appealing to Garvey.

'It is fitting you attended the party as Nelson, Nelligan,' said Knight.

'Nelson Nelligan? Got a ring to it.'

'As you may know, the Admiral's final signal to the fleet before the Battle of Trafalgar read thus: England

expects every man to do his duty. An admirable senti-
ment and a fitting epitaph for any great life. Nelson did
his duty in the times in which he lived. I intend to do
mine. Sadly for you, Nelligan, you will not be there to
see it.'

'Why? I'm going somewhere?'

'That,' smiled Bartholomew Knight, 'is entirely
dependent on my daughter. I have urgent matters to
attend to elsewhere. I leave you in Boudica's capable
hands.' He inclined his head. 'It has *not* been a pleasure.
Come.' He led his men away, Garvey lingering last and
sneering hatefully at Eddie as he went.

'Yeah, Frankie, don't give up on the facial remodelling
just yet.' And then there was only Boudica. With just the
two of them, it seemed easier to front her. 'I don't know
about you, but I didn't expect the evening to end up
quite like this.'

'Oh, Eddie. I'm sorry.' Boudica shook her head for-
lornly. 'I truly am. If you'd only been a SkyBike
mechanic for real, who knows? Who knows what kind of
future we might have had together?'

'We still can. It's not impossible.' Eddie preferred the
old-fashioned type of cell, the kind with bars that in vital
moments like this you could grab hold of and maybe
rattle and press your urgent face against. He was mildly
surprised that Knight hadn't kept them for reasons of
penal heritage. 'Boudica, listen to me. Your dad's obviously sick. Ill.' Deranged, he thought. 'If you help *me*, it's
not too late to help *him*. Come on. We meant something
to each other, you can't deny it. You can't just forget how
you feel.'

'I can, Eddie,' Boudica said simply. 'I have. But don't

worry. I think I may have already found a more deserv-
ing recipient for my affections. Your former colleague
Frankie Garvey seems nice.'

'No way,' Eddie despaired. 'Garvey?'

'You just don't get it, do you, Eddie?' Boudica sighed
like a disappointed teacher. 'It's not style or appearance
I'm interested in – I thought you might have guessed that
when I took up with you – it's passion, commitment,
belief in the cause. I am a Knight, Eddie. My first
loyalty is to my father. If he is ill, then the sickness flows
in my veins as well as his. And if you're not with us,
Eddie, you're against us.'

'Okay, Boudica.' Eddie shook his head in disappointed
defeat. There was no reaching her, no way back for her.
She was lost. 'Have it your way. So what are you planning on doing to a guy who's against you?'

'Oh, you'll find out,' Boudica laughed lightly, as if they
were discussing birthday surprises. 'Tomorrow. And I'd
get a good night's sleep in the meantime, Eddie,' she
advised. 'You're going to need *all* your strength.'

But of course, a good night's sleep was the last thing
Eddie got. Somehow, being locked up tended to play
havoc with his metabolism. He remembered reading
somewhere that in the old days of capital punishment in
Britain, the night before they were hanged the condemned men or women were given sleeping pills to get
them through the night. He'd always wondered what
would have happened had they overslept.

No chance of that in his case. It didn't help that now
and again Eddie felt sure he could hear a girl sobbing
nearby and knew that it was Rose. He called her name

but no reply came back. He'd have liked her still to have been in the cell with him. He would have held her, odd though she undoubtedly was. He felt she needed someone to hold her.

They were below ground, of course, so the only light they were allowed was artificial, and Eddie was permitted no watch to measure the passing of time. Spy High agents were trained to gauge it by natural means themselves, however, based on diagnosing the rhythms of their own bodies' daily cycles.

He was ready and waiting when Knight's men came for him.

'So what are you guys, then? The firing squad?' As he was escorted back up in the elevator, marched through the mansion. 'If it was gonna be shot at dawn like in the movies, I think you've missed it. What say we try again tomorrow?' There were four of them. He'd risk taking them all on only as a last resort. 'Knight obviously didn't employ you for your conversational abilities, did he?' The silence continued as his guard directed Eddie outside. 'What, without a jacket?' He was still wearing the shirt which, in less crumpled times, had been part of his Nelson costume. 'Or is this all part of the master plan? You're gonna tie me to a tree and wait 'til I freeze to death.'

'Ah, Eddie. Morning. How are you?'

Boudica. And not alone. She had half a dozen men with her. All seven of them were dressed in what Eddie recognised as the garb huntsmen had used to wear in the days before all blood-sports had been banned. Hunting pink, he thought it was called: scarlet coats, the cravats, the hard hats, the riding boots and jodhpurs. Boudica was differentiated from her companions not only by her sex but also because her coat was black, though the whole group looked as if it had stepped out of a documentary on aristocratic field pursuits of sixty years ago.

'Hi,' said Eddie. 'I think I'm as well as can be expected. Going for a ride, are we?'

'Going for a *hunt*,' Boudica said with relish, her dark eyes glittering.

Eddie had a bad feeling about that. 'I don't see any horses.'

'We don't need horses,' she said. 'Bring him.'

Eddie was led across the courtyard, to the edge of the lawns. Beyond those were forest. There'd be plenty of foxes and deer and other unsuspecting furry animals hiding out in there, Eddie thought, but he also suspected that Boudica's proposed quarry was already in plain view. As was her means of pursuit: seven customised SkyBikes all in a row, their colours and lines designed to resemble those of living horses instead of cold, metallic machines.

Boudica watched Eddie pale with pleasure. 'I see you've guessed what's in store for you, Eddie,' she gloated.

'If it's what I think it is, can't you just shoot me now and save us all a lot of trouble?'

'Oh, it'll be no trouble on our part.' As a child, she'd probably had a lot of fun plucking the legs from spiders. 'It's not often we can hunt these days. Foxes are a protected species, as I'm sure you know. Fortunately for us, the same protection does not extend to failed secret agents, and I've been itching to try out these new SkySteeds. These, too.' She crossed to her steed and retrieved from a slot in its side what looked like the handle of a sword but with no blade. 'We used to carry whips for our horses. Now we carry laser lashes for our prey.' An electric bolt of light crackled from the handle, perhaps a yard long, not stiff and straight like a conventional laser beam, but flexible, almost alive as Boudica twitched her hand. 'An interesting innovation, don't you think, Eddie?' she said. 'So much more adaptable.' The lash grew longer, hissed in the air. 'Yet sacrificing nothing in terms of the pain it can inflict.'

She struck out. The laser cut across Eddie's shoulders, sliced open his shirt. He gasped in burning, jolting agony, fell forward on to his knees. Heard the laughter and applause of Boudica's fellow huntsmen. This was bad. This was very bad. He didn't want to be taking too many blows like that. He wondered what the statistics for the survival rates of foxes had been in the old days.

'Get up, Eddie!' Boudica was demanding. 'Get up!' The lash fizzed and sparked at the gravel in front of him. 'We're going to hunt you down.'

'Like the dog I am?' Eddie managed a weak grin as he struggled to his feet. His shoulders felt like they were on fire.

'And try to put up some sort of show, will you?' Boudica said, mounting her SkySteed keenly. 'My friends and I are looking for good sport.'

'I hope I won't disappoint you,' Eddie muttered.

Spy High had trained its students always to identify the positive in any mission situation. Case in point: Eddie might have found himself herded across the lawns by seven psychopaths on SkySteeds and cracking laser lashes above his head, scorching and raising weals on his arms as he tried to protect his face and run at the same time, but at least they were leaving the four goons with shock blasters behind. At least Boudica *hadn't* elected simply to have him shot, as her father no doubt would have done. And at least, once they reached the forest, he'd have a chance to make off and lie low and think. They were pausing now, the huntsmen spreading out in a line with three on either side of Boudica, who leaned forward on her machine and gazed down at Eddie pitilessly. And only last night they'd been kissing.

'We're going to be sporting, too,' she said. 'We're going to give you five minutes' head start. But don't get too excited, Eddie. Don't think you'll be able to hide in a hollow and watch us fly by. Our steeds are equipped with heat-tracers. We'll know where you are at all times.'

SEVEN

Eddie pounded through the undergrowth. With him restricted to the ground and his hunters having access to the air, he wasn't going to be able to out-distance them for long. But that didn't mean he wasn't going to give it his best shot. First priority: find an area of low-hanging boughs and densely-packed trees – something to slow the SkySteeds down by forcing them into incessant manoeuvres. He vaulted fallen branches, leapt deceptive dips in the forest floor. Tried to maintain his speed. Tried to ignore the physical symptoms of distress, the screaming muscles, the gasping lungs. He didn't have time for pain.

His mind was racing, too. The only possible defence was attack. He had to turn the tables somehow. He had to convert hunters into hunted. But how?

He'd set off at a diagonal from Boudica's position on purpose. For several reasons. He didn't doubt that she was an expert on a SkySteed, and of all of his pursuers she had the greatest *personal* interest in making him suffer. Her scarlet-coated acolytes, however – what if *their* prime interest lay in impressing their employer, Bartholomew Knight's daughter? Could be a good word or even a promotion in it for them if they got to the fleeing spy first. They'd be eager to demonstrate their abilities, maybe *over*-eager. Eddie thought it best if he made an aspiring terrorist's day.

The deeper woodland fell away and suddenly he was in sunlight. An open stretch of grass that maybe once had been used as a track or something. A stand of oaks on the other side, ancient trees with tall, strong, mighty trunks. Perfect. He stopped, bent forward, forced his body to recover from the exertions so far. There would be more to come, but at least now he had his plan.

He jogged back a little the way he'd come, into the thicker forest where a SkySteed would have to curb its speed. And waited, taking deep breaths. Of course, if the huntsmen had already got behind him, it was obituary time. But they hadn't. *This* one hadn't, at any rate. The guy whose bike he could hear humming in the distance. The guy he could see flitting between the trees towards him.

Eddie thought he'd get him mad. He waved. 'Hi, what kept you?'

The huntsman clenched his teeth and gunned the engine.

Eddie ran.

He burst out on to the open ground again. Behind him the SkySteed cleared the foliage. He heard it. Surging. Closing. A whoop from the hunter. Dared to glance behind, to check the angle. The bike was slightly to his left, its rider cracking his laser lash in his right hand, preparing to strike out with it.

They were now just metres to the oaks.

Eddie hoped the clingboots worked as well in the field as they did in practice.

Scarcely breaking stride, he charged up the trunk of the oak. Heard the cry of astonishment from his pursuer as he veered his bike to avoid the tree.

He couldn't avoid Eddie.

Who jumped from the oak, twisting in the air like a gymnast. Who slammed into the huntsman, delivering a meaty right upper-cut to his jaw. Unseated, the hunter plunged to the ground.

The SkySteed was out of control, though, hurtling for collision with the oaks. Eddie reined it back, turned it sharply, desperately. The bark scraped his leg. He could live with that.

The huntsman was dazed but conscious, staggering to his feet. He recovered his senses just in time to see Eddie swooping towards him. Just in time to be aware of Eddie's fist. Clenched.

First stage of the fightback completed, Eddie thought. He wasn't celebrating. Premature triumphalism, like emotional involvement, was one of those weaknesses that could get an agent killed. He'd survived the latter so far by the skin of his teeth. Add the former as well and he'd be needing dentures. But he'd gained a SkySteed now. He'd stolen a laser lash. And Boudica's monitor screen would have shown the coming together of two flashing blips. Any second and she'd be —

'Is the quarry down? Come in. Talk to me. Has someone got him?'

Eddie flipped his communicator to send. ' 'Fraid not, Boudica. Quarry's still up. It's your man who's down. And now I'm coming for you.'

'Eddie? *Eddie!*'

He closed the channel on her rage. Stealth operations should always be conducted in silence.

But he wondered how she must be feeling, what orders she was barking to her remaining huntsmen. Watch out for him? Keep your eyes open? Stay in constant communication? Or maybe she thought he'd simply do a runner now that he had a SkySteed. If so, she soon realised that retreat was the last thing on his mind.

When Boudica realised she'd run out of allies, and that it was just her and Eddie, she made a hasty return to the mansion for more fire power.

Eddie got there first.

They faced each other like they were in the lists at a joust, their SkySteeds dappled in the woodland sunshine.

'Tell your friends thanks for the work-out, when they've regained consciousness,' called Eddie. 'It reminded me why I love this job so much. Now are you going to come quietly or what?'

'A Knight never surrenders,' Boudica glared. She activated her laser lash. It writhed in her hand like an electric serpent. Her steed reared as she rammed it into acceleration. 'Have at thee, varlet!'

'You what?' said Eddie, but he hurtled to meet her anyway.

She was whirling her lash above her head like a lasso. Going for a body shot. The need to punish him was clear and deadly in her eyes. Too emotional. Eddie had learned his lesson in that direction, as the SkySteeds closed, careered, converged, as his muscles tensed for action. Now it was Boudica's turn.

Her lash flailed sizzling through the air. Eddie leaned forward, took his bike low, whipped out with his own. Boudica missed him. Eddie did not miss. His target couldn't duck: the right propulsion unit of Boudica's SkySteed.

The laser shorted it out and the sudden absence of power on the right tipped the bike sideways. Boudica, already unbalanced in her obsession with lashing Eddie, floundered. With a cry of mingled outrage and fear, she fell. Thudded hard against the ground.

'Boudica!' Maybe, if the outcome had been reversed, the stricken girl would now have been crowing with delight at her enemy's defeat. Eddie didn't feel that way. Couldn't. He landed his bike and was by her side as quickly as possible. 'Boudica.' Unconscious. She'd be all right. Live to hunt another day. And it was strange, Eddie thought. All the hatred and the madness and the cruelty that he'd seen in her this morning, now it was all gone. If only it would never come back.

Eddie sighed, removed Boudica's riding hat and straightened her out on the grass, placed her hands across her chest, like one of those stone effigies of medieval ladies long ago entombed. Boudica was still warm, though. Eddie kissed her forehead, stroked her short, black hair. 'See you around, maybe.'

He'd noticed before the hunt began that several hover-limos were parked outside the mansion. One of those would serve as transport away from the grasp of Mr Bartholomew Knight. He had something else in mind for the SkySteed.

Eddie wasn't leaving here alone.

❖

He supposed he should have rung the bell or knocked or something similarly polite. Maybe even have waited for the butler. But he doubted that any of Knight's employees would have simply welcomed him back and shown him to the cells.

So he smashed through the mansion's doors on his SkySteed instead.

There was a goon in the hallway, one of the silent quartet from earlier. Eddie kept him quiet with a well-aimed blow of the laser lash. If only the bike was weapons grade, he could have blasted his way to Rose without any trouble. As it was, though, the element of surprise would have to do. A SkySteed steering wildly, hectically through the corridors couldn't have been a regular occurrence.

More of Knight's men rushed out of rooms, alerted by the shattering of the doors and the shouts of colleagues. Some were so stupefied they didn't even manage to get a shot off before Eddie felled them with the lash. Those that did proved to be poor marksmen, a deficiency they'd have the opportunity to rectify when they woke up.

Eddie crammed himself and the SkySteed into the guard-room elevator, pressed down. They'd be expecting him below, he guessed. A pity he'd have to disappoint them.

As the elevator doors opened, every one of Knight's guards opened fire. The SkySteed rampaged out at them regardless. Without a rider it couldn't get far, but it scattered the guards admirably before crashing into a bank of computers which promptly exploded.

'Where is he . . .? Put the fire out . . .! Where *is* he?'

Eddie was clingbooted to the elevator's ceiling. Now

he peeked into the guard-room. Saw the chaos. Saw his sleepshot wristbands. Thought he'd put the two together.

Eddie whistled.

A fusillade of shells eliminated virtually all the guards. The sleepshot penetrated clothing and skin, released its powerful anaesthetic into the men's bloodstreams instantaneously. The couple of survivors quickly succumbed to Eddie's laser lash.

'Rose? Rose!' He snapped on his wristbands, their addition to his weaponry boosting his confidence. A shock blaster in his hand and two thrust under his belt didn't do any harm, either. But none of it would matter if Knight had already moved her. 'Rose, it's Eddie! Answer me!'

'Eddie?' Her voice was uncertain.

He darted to the cells. There she was, sitting on the bed with her legs drawn up under her chin exactly as before. Perhaps her eyes seemed a *little* more interested in what was going on around her this time.

'Yep. Here's Eddie, back in your life again,' he grinned, extinguishing her cell's energy beams. 'You okay? Come on, I think it's time your accommodation was upgraded, don't you?'

Rose stood nervously, cast a dubious glance towards the guard-room. 'What about Mr Knight's men?'

'Put it this way. Mr Knight is not going to be pleased when they have to explain to him how they let us escape.'

'Are you going to take me to the project, Eddie?'

'Not yet,' he had to admit, aware of her increased anxiety as he did, 'but I'm gonna get you out, that's for sure.'

'Out?'

He didn't think he ought to trust her with a blaster. 'Just keep behind me, Rose. Keep right behind me. There might be some fighting to do yet.'

Though not in the guard-room. The computers burned quietly but otherwise all was still. Eddie led Rose into the elevator, which she seemed to be regarding with suspicion. If they could break out into the mansion in one piece, he reckoned they'd make it. The elevator started to rise. Rose started to breath more quickly. There was panic in her eyes.

'It's okay,' Eddie reassured her. 'Knight's goons couldn't catch a cold between them, let alone us. I'm not going to let anything happen to you.'

'But,' and this seemed to be a cause of inexplicable fear for her, 'we're going *up*.'

There was no time to ask why this was a problem. 'To the side!' The elevator doors slid open. A solitary shock blast struck the rear wall, further scarring the already pock-marked metal. Eddie judged the trajectory of the shot, stabbed his arm out and fired sleepshot. Direct hit. The lackey sagged to the floor with the faint sigh of someone in slumber.

'We're gonna make a run for it now,' warned Eddie. 'Remember what I said, Rose. Stay right behind me.'

He couldn't see her face as they raced through the mansion's by now almost familiar corridors, but he wouldn't have been surprised if it was terror-stricken. It would have been a normal reaction to the bodies of the unconscious goons which still lay where Eddie had left them on his way in. There were two more on the main staircase, but very much awake, their shock blasts charring Bartholomew Knight's beautifully polished floor.

Eddie elected to use one of his own blasters this time, set to Materials. The staircase erupted, pitching those using it as cover into the hall.

Rose was clinging on to his arm. Her fingers digging like claws. 'Eddie, no!'

He'd been right – she was panic-stricken. 'It's okay,' he encouraged. 'I think that's the last of them. Come on. Our transport awaits.'

The entrance with its splintered doors was like a mouth full of broken teeth. But beyond it, escape and safety beckoned.

Eddie moved forward. Rose tried to hold him back. Her hands gripped his arm so tightly they were almost threatening his circulation. She was *more* frightened now, not less, her gaze fixed on the outside.

'What's the matter? Rose, we've got to move. If they've contacted reinforcements . . .'

'No. Eddie. *Outside.*'

'Where we need to go. Now.' There wasn't time for this. He virtually pulled her with him. Across the hall. To the doorway. Through it.

Despite everything, it was a rather pleasant day.

Rose screamed. As they exited the mansion, she screamed with such total, almost primal terror that instinctively Eddie flinched away. She flung her arms up to protect her face. She shrunk back, crumbled, collapsed on the gravel of the courtyard.

'No, Eddie, please! Take it away! Take it *away*!'

It was something above her. The source of her terror was above her. Eddie gazed upwards.

The sky.

❖

'She's quieter now, Master Edward. I have administered a mild sedative.'

'Thanks, Bowler.' Eddie exhaled and shook his head. *'That's* something I don't want to have to go through again. I virtually had to carry her to the limo. Once we got inside, once there was a roof over her head she wasn't so bad, but . . . is she a major league agoraphobic or what, Bowler? Exactly who is she?'

'I have taken the liberty of sending the young lady's name and physical details to the Deveraux College, Master Edward. If any information about her at all is stored in our computer systems, we shall soon know.' He paused. 'I have also communicated to Mr Deveraux an advance report of your experience at the Knight mansion. It is felt that with the integrity of your cover story compromised, it might be dangerous to remain here. Mr Deveraux recommends we relocate to our address in Westminster immediately.'

'No chance,' dismissed Eddie. 'Not until Rose has had time to recover. We're not moving her again until she's up to it.'

Bowler permitted his eyebrows to rise just above the normal. By his reserved standards, the equivalent to eye-bulging, jaw-dropping astonishment for most people. 'Master Edward,' he said, entirely without inflection, 'may I reintroduce two words not utterly irrelevant to the present situation. Emotional and involvement.'

'No, Bowler,' said Eddie, with plenty of inflection, all of it irritated, 'you may not. What you may do is get back to Deveraux and say we'll move in the morning. Nothing's going to happen tonight. Now, I'm going to speak to Rose, okay?'

'Very well, Master Edward,' consented Bowler, and his expression didn't change even when Eddie was no longer looking at it.

Rose was in his bedroom, in his bed. They'd darkened the windows to full black so there was no chance of her being able to peer out and see rooftops and sky and space. After their escape from Knight's mansion, Eddie had driven hard to get them back home to Camden Town. There'd been no sign of pursuit but he knew that Bowler and Deveraux were actually right. The flat could no longer be considered secure. Boudica had sent a limo for him the other day. It was only to be hoped that with his mansion penetrated and his own position exposed, Bartholomew Knight had more on his mind than the possible whereabouts of Eddie and Rose.

'Hi. Are you awake?' Dumb question, really. He might have guessed she'd be sitting with her legs drawn up under her chin.

'Eddie.' She seemed pleased to see him. She'd had a shower since arriving at the apartment. Her hair was now stunningly red. 'You're funny.'

'Is that funny peculiar or funny ha-ha?' Rose looked blank. 'It doesn't matter. Do the pyjamas fit okay?' She was wearing a pair of Eddie's own. 'I mean, I could always help adjust them if . . . okay, no. We've got to be serious. Rose, can I ask you some questions?'

'Of course. What about?'

'About you.' He pulled up a chair to her bedside. 'I don't want to come on like some sort of interrogator, but I do think there are one or two things we need to establish if we can.'

'I'm Rose Warwick. I've already told you that.'

'Yeah. Other than that. What about your extreme reaction to the sky, Rose. Can you tell me about that?'

She glanced warily at the black rectangle of the window. 'It's so big. It goes on for ever. It makes me feel like I don't matter at all, like I'm a speck of dust.' She looked back at Eddie. 'I'd never seen it before.'

'What?' If he'd been Bowler, Eddie's eyebrows would now be on the top of his head.

'Not until recently. Not until Mr Knight came.'

'Where?'

'To the project.'

'That's where you live? The Pendragon Project?'

'I thought you already knew that.'

'Only by guesswork,' Eddie conceded, 'but I *want* to know more.' Rose's world was drawing him in. 'Tell me about the Pendragon Project, Rose. Where is it? What is it?'

'I don't know where it is,' she said mournfully. 'Its location is one of its greatest secrets. I'm not sure I should even be talking about it, Eddie. But I trust you. I think you can help me.'

'I want to help you.'

'I'm glad. And the reason you won't have heard of the Pendragon Project or ever have seen it is because it's underground. I live underground, Eddie, in a wonderful place of metal skies and eternal light. I'm learning to be a scientist there like my father. Not that that's unexpected or unusual. Everyone's a scientist in the project. That's what we're for. But my father is Henry Warwick our Head Scientist and Project Leader, which makes him the most important person there.' She spoke proudly. 'And you don't have to be his

daughter to see he deserves to be. He invents such marvellous weapons.'

'Say again?' For a moment, Eddie had thought Rose
was waxing lyrical about weaponry.

'That's what we do, Eddie,' Rose confirmed without
shame. 'That's what our forefathers were chosen to do. It
is our noble purpose. We create weapons for the day of
Britain's need.'

Eddie was beginning to see why Bartholomew Knight
might be interested in Rose Warwick.

'And *every* day, we gather in the Great Chamber before
work period starts, and we sing hymns and we say
prayers and my father tells us whether this day is *The*
Day, whether the Britain that none of us has ever seen,
the Britain of the surface world, has called on us at last.
And until Bartholomew Knight, it never had.'

'Knight came to the Pendragon Project?'

'At first, when my father heard his voice through the
communicator and learned that our long wait was finally
over, he seemed glad. We all did. Work period was abandoned for the day to celebrate. Our exile was almost at
an end. Then I found my father in his living-booth and
he was crying and I asked him why. He said lately he'd
had doubts about our work, when he thought about the
stockpiles of death we'd created over the long decades.
He said he was worried what kind of England now
existed above our heads, what kind of Englishman
would soon possess the power to use our weapons
against an enemy, for the good of the country. And he
said he was afraid, because after living his whole life in
the project, now that the time of its fulfilment was upon
him, he realised that he could not be certain what the

good of the country *was* any more. Would the fruits of his labour *save* England or *destroy* it? And I hugged my father then and he hugged me and he told me that whatever happened no harm would come to me. I was his daughter and he loved me. It was the last time I held my father. The next day, Bartholomew Knight arrived.'

Eddie was torn. He really ought to let Deveraux know about this immediately. He was pretty sure that Henry Warwick and Co might have had something to do with the swarm-shells that had destroyed the Channel Bridge. But at the same time, he couldn't leave Rose's story before it was finished. She'd spent her *whole* life underground? No wonder she was so pale.

'I never liked Bartholomew Knight,' she was continuing, 'not from the first moment I saw him. While everyone else was clamouring around the surface people as my father led them into the Great Chamber, I saw his eyes, and I saw madness there. And coldness. I knew that he would have no hesitation in using our inventions against whomever he chose. The men who accompanied him, they carried guns. Two of them, the men who kept closest to Knight's side, were taller than the others, but they all looked grim, dangerous. They all wore strange clothes. What kind of world had they left to enter ours?

'To begin with all was well. Bartholomew Knight satisfied my father that the time of crisis was indeed at hand. He said that England had fallen into decadence and corruption and was beleaguered by her enemies on all sides, her very survival as a nation endangered. He thanked my father and his fellow scientists for their sacrifices, praised them as patriots, as heroes. He demanded to be shown the weapons we had made. And my father showed him.

'That night they came for me in my living-booth, Bartholomew Knight and his two giants. They told me to get dressed but I refused. They told me again and said that if I disobeyed I would never see my father alive again. And Bartholomew Knight told me that he always meant what he said.'

Rose's voice was becoming more emotional as she relived her ordeal in her mind. 'They took me away. They said it was for my own good and for my father's good. They said it might help him to cooperate. I didn't see him. They didn't let me see him. They took me where I'd never been before, beyond the Seal, into tunnels that were dark, and I was frightened but they didn't care. We went up in a lift – they called it an elevator – and then they took me on to the surface. Outside.' She pressed her forehead against her knees, clenching her eyelids closed as though trying to shut out the past. 'It wasn't my fault. I couldn't help it, Eddie. I'd never seen such . . . hugeness. I couldn't have believed it. The surface world, it was limitless. It was infinite. It terrified me. So I screamed. And I was sick. But they didn't care.'

'And they took you to Knight's mansion? You've been in the cells ever since?' Rose nodded meekly. 'For how long, Rose? Do you know?'

'Longer than days. A few weeks, I think. I tried to cope. I tried to imagine I was a scientist in a new environment that I needed to analyse and learn as much about as possible, but it didn't work then and it's not working now. Eddie, I want to see my father again. I want to go home.'

'I know,' soothed Eddie. If her father was still alive. If Knight hadn't already torched the Pendragon Project.

'But I don't know how to find it,' Rose lamented. 'I don't know how to get back.'

'We'll find it.' Eddie hugged her consolingly. She rested her head against him. He nearly kissed her hair. 'I promise. I'll look after you.'

'Thank you, Eddie.'

'No worries,' said Eddie. 'Now you just try and get some sleep.' There was much he needed to tell Bowler. 'You're safe here.'

'Promise that, too?'

Eddie was about to.

But then the window exploded.

EIGHT

The room was suddenly jagged with glass, gleaming shards slicing for Eddie's head.

'Get down!' He instinctively shielded Rose as a blaze of laser fire erupted through the gaping window. Then, as the laser fire paused he pulled her down to shelter behind the bed. Her eyes were wild with fright but she did not scream. She was looking at Eddie as if she trusted him to keep them both safe. He thought it might be a good idea if he did.

They were Jacks. On lines hanging from somewhere above. They wore helmets and body armour but the flags on their faces could not be mistaken. The first pair were already swinging through the opening, disengaging themselves from their cables and raking the room with their laser rifles.

Luckily, Eddie was still wearing his sleepshot wristbands. And even pinned down his aim was perfect.

'Why can't you guys just knock like everyone else?' he complained as he drilled sleepshot shells through the Jacks' body armour, stopped them in their tracks.

At least they were in the right place if they wanted a nap.

'Eddie, there's more of them!' Rose clutched at his shoulder.

Her observational skills had clearly not been stunted by a lifetime in the Pendragon Project. She was right. As quickly as Eddie sent the Jacks into slumberland, reinforcements dangled outside the window craving access. They weren't abseiling from the roof. They had to be being lowered from a transport.

Eddie glanced to the door as their sheltering bed started to burn. Did he dare risk a run for it? They couldn't stay here for much longer.

The door burst open. Bowler stood in the doorway. He was dressed as impeccably as ever, his cufflinks polished, his jacket and trousers neatly pressed, the top button of his shirt done up. He held a stun rifle under each arm and mowed the Jacks down as if he was polishing the silver. The force of the stun blaster thudded the invaders off their feet, propelled several back the way they'd come in, and now they were no longer attached to their cables. Gravity was on the side of the good.

'Might one suggest we retire to the weapons centre, Master Edward?' Bowler said, not unreasonably.

'Bowler, if you weren't an older man and if I didn't have a reputation to uphold, I'd kiss you!'

'Master Edward, please, a professional secret agent must keep cool and thoughtful in times of stress. After you, Miss Warwick.'

Eddie couldn't let Bowler have *all* the fun. Even as he and Rose darted for the door, he managed to get a final spray of sleepshot in.

The three of them fell back towards the weapons centre. The apartment was shuddering with further explosions as the Jacks sought entry through the door as well as the window. The automatic Intruder Electrification System would delay them for a while, but not indefinitely.

'It's a full scale assault,' Eddie said.

'Indeed, Master Edward. I believe the phrase in common parlance is that they are coming out of the woodwork.'

'Then we need to defumigate. Bowler, can you deal with the guys already inside while I . . .' Eddie jabbed a finger upwards.

A clutch of Jacks charged into the corridor, baying for blood. Bowler shot them down almost primly. 'Oh, I think so, Master Edward.'

'Great.' He squeezed Rose's hand briefly. 'Stay with Bowler.'

'Eddie, where . . .?'

'Don't worry,' he grinned. 'As they used to say in the movies, I'll be back.'

Through the lab, past the holo-gym, the sound of gunfire pursuing him. He had to be quick. Not even Bowler could hold out for ever. He made for the SkyBike bay. Eddie leapt into the saddle like a cowboy on to a horse, flipped the controls alongside him. Instantly, hidden hydraulics raised the platform on which the SkyBike was mounted. As they did so, the facing wall slid open, granting a panoramic view of the London skyline, nothing between Eddie and it but space.

He booted up the magnetic core. The propulsion units whirred. Weapons systems fully operational. A

Deveraux issue SkyBike put even a Zero Mark Three to shame.

Bracing himself for action, Eddie shot out into the night.

In the streets below, some sort of minor riot seemed to be in progress. People were fleeing in panic from a gang of Jacks, fully flagged and garbed in their more traditional uniform of boots and denim, and doing what they apparently did best – destroying stuff. The smashing of glass and the crackle of burning wheellesses rose on the air currents to Eddie's ears, mingling with the screams of the public. And what was the police helicopter hovering above his building like an ugly black insect doing about it? Nothing good. Nobody would question the presence of such an aircraft at a scene of social unrest. And mid-riot, no one would spot that it wasn't a police helicopter at all, even with a final handful of Jacks still visible through its open side-doors and preparing to leap from their lines. The riot was a diversion while Knight's shock troops attacked Eddie's flat. Well, he'd have to leave them to Bowler. His immediate priority was to give the chopper's pilot something to think about.

A burst of laser fire at his rear rotors, for example.

Flames plumed and the helicopter wobbled in the air. The remaining Jacks crouched inside, still hooked on to their cables, and directed their weapons at the rogue SkyBike. Eddie snorted in derision. They were slow motion to him, statues. He swooped, raking the chopper's exposed flank with his lasers, scoring deep ruts in the metal, then fired a stun grenade into its innards. Jacks went sprawling.

The pilot panicked.

The chopper veered higher, slanting away from Eddie's building, abandoning those men already committed to the fray. Somebody dived from the craft as if keen to join them, and was left swinging from the end of his line like a manic pendulum or a suicidal bungee jumper, his few conscious comrades desperately trying to reel him back in. From full scale assault to full scale retreat. Eddie could shoot the helicopter out of the sky if he wanted to, but if he did that the machine would crash down on the heads of innocent Londoners, and even Jonathan Deveraux might have a problem explaining that away. Or he could pursue the fleeing chopper, follow it back to its base, maybe find Bartholomew Knight himself all nice and ready to be arrested. But there was no way he could do that, either. Eddie braked his SkyBike as the helicopter flew into distant darkness. Bowler and Rose needed him first. The bad guys would have to wait.

Though as it turned out, he could maybe have followed the Jacks after all. His apartment looked no worse than if he'd held a very wild party: furniture wrecked, gate-crashers groaning on the floor in semi-conscious heaps and a parent figure standing aloofly disapproving in the middle of it all.

Rose rushed gladly towards him. 'Eddie, you're all right!' She flung her thin arms around him.

'I won't be if you suffocate me,' he gasped. But when she let him go he was sorry. 'Everything under control, Bowler?'

'I believe so, Master Edward, though I fear I may have a powder burn on my sleeve. I do apologise.'

'What are you talking about?' Eddie laughed. 'It's *me* who should apologise. If I'd listened to you about switching safe-houses earlier, this whole battle could have been avoided. The Jacks staged a riot to cover their little attempt at siege warfare – false police helicopter and everything. When the *real* cops arrive we'll have some explaining to do.'

'The Deveraux organisation will settle matters with the local law enforcement agencies, Master Edward,' said Bowler. 'You need not concern yourself about that. But it seems clear we have little choice now but to relocate.'

'Westminster?'

Bowler considered. 'I feel it might be wise to go a little further than that for the moment,' he advised. 'Spy High.'

It was the same as always, yet somehow it was different.

The gothic façade of the Deveraux College seemed unaltered from the day Eddie had first glimpsed it. He'd been fourteen then, and he hadn't known that the students engaged in silent struggles on the football field, the students who were still there, still playing in a remarkable show of stamina, were not flesh and blood boys at all, but holograms designed to project an image of educational normality.

'Why?' Rose asked interestedly as Eddie led her inside.

'It's a disguise,' he explained. 'So nobody guesses what *really* goes on here.'

Rose nodded. She was better indoors, more confident with a good solid roof over her head, and you couldn't get more good and solid than Deveraux's re-inforced missile-resistant outer shell. Indoors, it was easier for her to exchange fear of the unknown for scientific curiosity in this strange new surface world and its technology.

'And this isn't a study, either,' she said in fascination as the two of them entered a desk-dominated, book-lined room that very much appeared to be so. 'At least, not primarily.'

'Exactly,' said Eddie. 'Its main function is a lot more fun. It's an elevator. We've got several others like it. They all take us down below ground to the hi-tech heart of our operation, to where Spy High truly begins.'

'Down, below and ground.' Rose smiled self-deprecatingly. 'My three favourite words. How does it work?'

'Just push in the spine of that book there.'

'"Diamonds Are Forever"?'

'That's the one.'

He watched her do it. Eddie was relieved, if surprised, that he'd been allowed to bring Rose to Deveraux without the slightest hint that there could be a mind-wipe awaiting her at the end of it. Rose's unique upbringing made her different from the norm, an exception to any rule. And Jonathan Deveraux always had a *thing* about exceptions.

'Are we there yet?' asked Rose impatiently, like a child on a journey.

'Open the door and see,' invited Eddie.

Rose did. Rose saw. 'Oh, *Eddie*.' And Rose evidently approved.

But even while he was both pleased and amused by his companion's open-mouthed rapture, Eddie could not feel entirely happy. Here, amidst the familiarity of his surroundings, he still felt that something was missing. As he showed Rose the old rooms, the Intelligence Gathering Centre, the virtual reality chamber complete with cyber-cradles, he realised what it was. *Who* it was. His old team-mates. Cally, Bex, Ben, Jake and Lori. Bond Team. Eddie didn't recognise any of the kids here now. The ones who were scurrying between lessons, looking so young and in ShockSuits that seemed several sizes too big for them.

The place was the same yet different.

'Eddie, are you all right?' Rose was gazing at him with concern.

'Sure. Why wouldn't I be?' He laughed a little falsely. 'Just waiting for Mr Korita or Ms Bannon or somebody to appear out of nowhere and remind me I've still got an assignment due, just like the old days.'

'I know about the old days, Eddie,' said Rose. 'In the project they were all we had.' She squeezed his hand comfortingly.

'Let go of him at once, girl! You don't know where he's been!'

Eddie turned, scarcely believing his ears. It wasn't a member of the faculty appearing out of nowhere. Better than that. It was Bex.

'Still in one piece, Eddie?' She grinned. 'I was sure the bad guys would have got you by now. Don't take this as a sign that I've been pining for you, but how about a hug?'

'A hug, Bex?' Eddie opened his arms wide. 'I'd hoped for at least a massage.'

'Same old Eddie.' The two of them embraced, Eddie

receiving a mouthful of spiky pink hair by way of a bonus.

'Same old Bex.'

'And I guess this must be Rose.' Offering her hand which the other girl took shyly and fleetingly. 'News travels fast in our line of work. Hi. I'm Bex Deveraux.'

'Rose Warwick. I'm pleased to meet you.'

'You'd be the first,' quipped Eddie. 'But don't be put off by all the piercings and the hairstyle from hell. When it comes down to it, Bex is actually rather normal.'

'Yeah,' grinned Bex, 'and when it comes down to it, Eddie actually rather isn't.'

'*I* think he is,' Rose said simply, evidently uninitiated in the rituals of ironic banter. 'I think he's nice.'

'You think Eddie's nice?' Bex feigned horror. 'Girl, have *you* got a lot to learn.'

Bex led them to the rec room, where she loaned Rose a hand-held videvision unit tuned into the World Now channel. As the girl from the Pendragon Project began her education in the affairs of the surface, the two former Bond Teamers caught up on the latest gossip.

'No, Eddie,' Bex corrected him, 'I didn't come running as soon as I heard you were popping back to Spy High. I was already here, seeing my dad – taking a little R and R between missions.'

'I'm honoured.'

'So you should be. And I'm envious. This Pendragon thing sounds like a real winner. Me, I've only had DNA-smugglers and mutant cyborgs to deal with. Oh, and a guy who planned on using alien technology to ascend to godhood.'

'What happened to him?'

'He ascended to a penal satellite instead.'

Eddie chuckled. 'Have you heard from the others?'

'Not much,' Bex admitted. 'I don't know about you, Ed, but Bond Team sure seems a long time ago to me.'

'I know what you mean. I was feeling the same.'

'I spoke to Lori a while back. Did you know she and Jake have split up?'

'What?' Eddie was shocked. After all the friction there had been between Jake and Ben over who was the right boy for Lori, he couldn't believe she wasn't with either of them. 'What happened?'

'She wouldn't say, but from the sound of things it wasn't what you'd call an amicable parting of the ways.'

'Who'd have believed it? I guess that's the thing about relationships, though, isn't it. They're like tomorrow. You never know what they're gonna bring.'

'Excuse me while I just close my eyes and commune with the profundity of that statement, O Wise One,' said Bex.

'I'd thought about getting in touch with Jake as well,' Eddie reflected. 'Thought as he was a Domer he might have been able to help Rose adjust to her new life on the surface. Thought he'd maybe understand what she might be going through better than me. Perhaps I'll give it a miss though now, Bex, what do you think?'

'I think you'll be all the help for Rose she'll need, Eddie,' Bex said.

'Okay, there's no need to mock.'

'I wasn't mocking.'

Eddie dismissed the subject. 'You know, going back to Lori and Jake, I mean, maybe it's kind of like the Curse of Bond Team. We're doomed never to find the right relationship. You know what I mean? I mean, the number of times things haven't worked out since we all joined Spy High.'

'Where is this heading, Eddie?' Bex said cautiously. 'You're not planning on embarrassing yourself, are you?'

'No,' denied Eddie. 'I'm just saying, I wonder what would have happened if we'd . . . you know, *tried*.'

'Any chances we had are in the past, Eddie,' Bex said, 'and if you look for relationships in the past you'll end up lonely. It's the future you want.' Bex leaned forward confidentially and whispered 'And I reckon she's the one sitting beside you with the red hair.'

'What? Bex?' He mouthed her name. 'Rose?'

But there was no time to pursue the matter. A metallic voice announced over the tannoy that Mr Deveraux would like to see Edward Nelligan in his rooms at once. Bex sighed. 'How come I never get the same summons?'

'Listen, Bex, we'll talk again later, yeah?'

'You're not going, Eddie?' Rose looked up from her videvision.

'Yeah.' He frowned, uncertain what to say or do. 'Rose, I think . . .'

'I'll look after Rose, Ed,' offered Bex, slipping her arm around the other girl's shoulders. 'And don't worry. I'll only tell her *all* your secrets.'

'Okay.' Eddie stood awkwardly. 'I'd better . . . you'll be all right with Bex, Rose?'

'Oh, I think so,' beamed Rose.

'Right, well, I'll be back as quick as I can.' Eddie regarded both girls, seemed puzzled. 'Bye.' Spoken reluctantly. But nobody kept Jonathan Deveraux waiting.

```
IGC DATA-FILE 2066
SUB-SECTION: GREAT BRITAIN MEDIA FEED
```

Social unrest has not only continued but increased ahead of the Treaty of Europa Conference to be held in London in ten days' time. Besides the capital itself, riots have rocked the centres of major cities from Liverpool and Leeds to Southampton and Bristol, while the hooligan element known as the Jacks have been at the centre of a nationwide wave of violent protest.

Prime Minister Peregrine Barnes has condemned the disturbances as anti-democratic as well as anti-social, and has called on UK First Party leader Bartholomew Knight to do the same. Mr Knight, however, has made no statement about the disorder and has not been seen in public for several days.

Meanwhile, Albion has reiterated its warning that it will not permit the conference to go ahead, and that any attempt on the part of the authorities to persist will result in severe consequences. Exactly what those consequences might be, however, remains to be seen.

Whenever he entered Jonathan Deveraux's rooms, which admittedly was not often (they weren't exactly a drop by for a coffee and a bit of a chat venue) Eddie expected to see Senior Tutor Elmore Grant there, the man who'd guided him and the rest of Bond Team through their training. These days, though, that wasn't going to happen, largely because Grant was now *former*

Senior Tutor. He was retired and another man was sitting in his study and running his hands through prematurely greying hair. Another reason why Spy High no longer seemed quite the same.

Deveraux himself, however, was a constant – computer programs tended not to age – and Eddie was pleased to find Bowler in residence as well. A little bit of human solidarity in the face of the founder's unblinking stare.

'So, it seems our suspect has vanished,' Deveraux's image said from the screen. 'Following your encounter with him, Agent Nelligan, we have taken steps to confiscate and appropriate all Bartholomew Knight's known holdings and businesses. His mansion, Little England and a range of other establishments, all are now in our hands, and none have supplied us with any clue as to where the man himself might be hiding.'

'Computer records, sir?' suggested Eddie.

'Wiped clean,' said Deveraux. 'Knight has covered his tracks extremely proficiently.'

'What about Boudica?' He tried to sound disinterested – after all, how could you care what happened to someone who just the other day had tried to kill you, even if said someone was gorgeous? – but he was aware that Bowler was regarding him closely. 'Any sign of her? Have we checked out the country's riding schools?'

'Boudica Knight is as elusive as her father,' Deveraux conceded, 'but we must proceed on the basis that their threat to the Europa Conference is real. Whether they call themselves Albion or whether they do not, as long as the Knights have access to the weaponry produced by the Pendragon Project the danger to order they pose must be treated with the utmost seriousness.'

'Absolutely,' agreed Eddie vigorously. 'So what's our move? I mean, sir?'

'We must locate the Pendragon Project itself,' Deveraux decided. 'By doing so, it is also highly likely that we will discover the whereabouts of Bartholomew Knight.'

Eddie frowned. 'A good plan, sir, but there's a bit of a problem. Nobody knows where the Pendragon Project is.'

'Rose Warwick knows,' Deveraux said with confidence.

'Ah . . .' Far be it for a humble field agent to contradict the founder of Spy High, but Eddie didn't think he really had a lot of choice. 'Actually, sir, I'm not sure she does . . .'

'She knows.' Jonathan Deveraux's image multiplied on the screens as if to carry the argument by sheer weight of numbers. 'Even if that knowledge is not conscious. The human brain, Agent Nelligan, is an impressive piece of software. It records every single experience in its owner's life with infallible accuracy. It stores in its neural circuits, in its synapses and cells and lobes, the memories, emotions and ideas of a lifetime. The individual human being may not be able to access them all – humans use only a fraction of the power of their brains – but the information exists nonetheless.'

'But, sir,' groped Eddie, aware that he was probably accessing only a *very* small fraction of the power of *his* brain, 'if we can't remember the relevant material, I mean, if Rose can't remember how to find the Pendragon Project, even if that's lodged in her mind somewhere, how does that help us?'

'It helps us, Agent Nelligan,' said Jonathan Deveraux, 'because we now possess the technology to *dis*lodge such information from Rose Warwick's brain. The Deveraux organisation is now able to open up any human brain for our inspection.'

'What?' Eddie felt a sudden revulsion. 'You mean surgery?'

'Nothing so crude, Agent Nelligan,' assured Deveraux. 'Rose Warwick simply has an appointment with the Mindwinder.'

'I suppose I can put this down as another first, Eddie, can't I?' Clad now in a regulation Spy High shocksuit, its silver material contrasting dramatically with her tide of red hair, Rose appeared slimmer and more vulnerable than ever. She was holding his hands and not wanting to let go; the feeling seemed mutual. 'From a purely scientific point of view it's going to be an experience. But safety . . .'

'You'll be fine. Trust me. It's not even gonna tickle.' He glanced down at the cyber-cradle awaiting Rose's entry. 'Me and Bex have been in these things dozens of times, isn't that right, Bex?'

'That's right,' said Bex. She and Eddie also wore shocksuits, and two more of the virtual reality chamber's cyber-cradles were primed for immediate use.

'Not the same one at the same time, of course,' Eddie grinned. 'That'd be a bit of a squeeze, if you know what I mean.'

'Eddie.' Rose shook her head, managed the mildest of smiles.

'But honestly, Rose, there's nothing to worry about.

The Mindwinder program is just going to allow us to examine your memories of being brought to Knight's mansion from the project. I guess it's a bit like hypnotism without the "look into my eyes" and "you are feeling sleepy", more kind of high-tech.'

'But I don't know the names of any of the places,' Rose said helplessly.

'You don't need to,' Bex stepped in. 'As soon as the Mindwinder's identified and visualised the appropriate memories, those images will be compared with Great Britain's geography until a match is found. Once that's done, we'll be able to use our satellite systems to pinpoint the project as easily and accurately as Eddie here can find his mouth at meal-times.'

'And then,' hopefully, 'I can see my father again?'

Bex turned to Eddie. 'I hope so,' he said. He saw the techs ready to begin the transference process. 'Okay, let's get it done.' He helped Rose into the cyber-cradle. 'And remember, Rose, Bex and me'll be in your memories with you.'

'I know.' She sat down on the cradle's leather cushioning, gave Eddie one final, frightened hug. 'So do I just lie back?'

'That's right. Stretch yourself out. Make yourself comfortable.'

But Rose didn't *look* comfortable. Not as the techs took over and strapped her in, like a crash test dummy. Not as her pleading eyes didn't waver once from Eddie as the virtual sensors pressed like cold fingers against her temples. And particularly not as the cyber-cradle's glass shield descended upon her, clicking into place and sealing her off from the real world, the organic world –

preparing her for transfer to virtual reality, to the Mindwinder. Reluctantly, Rose closed her eyes. The cradle hummed her to sleep like a cybernetic lullaby. Only now did she appear at rest.

'Pretty as a picture,' Bex observed. 'Fancy getting inside her head, Ed?'

'You have such a beautiful turn of phrase, Bex,' Eddie admired ironically. 'But I guess so. And hey, joking apart—'

'Joking *apart*? I thought you were the Eddie Nelligan who used to be in Bond Team?'

'Oh, ho, ho. No, Bex. Joking apart – *thanks*. For staying around for the Mindwinder. I appreciate the moral support.' A frown flickered across Eddie's face. 'I know I told Rose everything would be cool, and I know your dad's never wrong, and if he says the Mindwinder's safe and it'll work, then it's safe and it'll work . . .'

'But *still*,' said Bex.

'Yeah.' Old friends always understood. 'Still.'

'We'd like to begin, Agent Nelligan, Agent Deveraux.' The techs were growing restless.

Eddie thought about the Mindwinder as he secured himself inside a cradle and instructed his body to relax. The technology, as far as he'd understood Jonathan Deveraux's polysyllabic explanation, was a combination between a state of the art virtual reality program and the kind of organic-cybernetic interface that had allowed Deveraux's own personality and brain patterns to be preserved intact when his human body perished. The stuff of Rose's mind was going to be rendered three-dimensionally, and they were going to be able to rifle through her memories, rewinding her life and then fast-forwarding it again like some kind of living DVD. Bypass the boring parts, playback the excitement – the Mindwinder program could reduce a life to entertainment. And that kind of bothered Eddie, even as his transference into Rose's consciousness commenced. Was it really moral to probe another human being's mind like this, even with their consent, even if doing so could help save lives? Lori had always been the one big on Ethics in Espionage issues; Eddie'd always just liked shooting guns and flying SkyBikes. In any case, there was no time to dwell on the matter now. The shield was closed and Eddie already felt the virtual reality chamber slipping away, his body with it.

Or no. Maybe not. He was standing in the chamber again and the techs were still preparing the three cyber-cradles. Bex was at his shoulder. She was also a little ahead of him, as was Rose and, most perplexing of all, himself. An Eddie he recognised as such but who somehow seemed bigger, stronger, better-looking than the eighteen-year-old who mugged him from his mirror several times a day.

'I suppose I can put this down as another first, Eddie, can't I?' Rose was addressing his more manly twin, holding his hands and not wanting to let go.

'What's this?' Eddie queried.

'It's Mindwinder.' The Bex at his side gazed around in wonderment. 'Don't you see, Eddie? It's worked. We're inside Rose's most recent memory, immediately before she's placed in the cyber-cradle.'

Eddie watched himself comforting Rose. 'How come they can't see us?'

'I guess because we weren't part of the original moment, not the two of us standing here, I mean.'

'I didn't look quite like that *in* the original moment,' Eddie pointed out. 'I only wish I did. I could maybe start a second career as a model.'

Bex laughed. 'Eddie you idiot, you *do* look like that. To Rose. This isn't objective reality, it's Rose's version of the world, her individual interpretation of it reflected through her own memories. That's how Rose sees you, Eddie.'

'It is?' The flame-haired, heroic figure counselling Rose that there was honestly nothing to worry about humbled Eddie. He didn't feel worthy. 'That guy is me?'

'Yep. And does *Rose* need optical implants like now.' Bex tipped Eddie a wink. 'But didn't I try to tell you earlier? She likes you, Eddie. Rose likes you. She's the one. And it's obvious you like her. That matching red hair's a giveaway, isn't it? Go for it.'

Eddie half-smiled, half-frowned. Was Bex on the button? Had the Right Girl come along after all, just when he least expected it? He shook his head. Anyone would think he was living in a novel.

A voice that wasn't part of the scene sounded in his ears. Deveraux. 'Your acclimatisation period is over, Agents Nelligan and Deveraux.' As clinical as ever. Eddie didn't dare ask Bex what it felt like to be called Agent Deveraux by your father. He imagined it wasn't special. 'Stand by for mindwind.'

And suddenly there was movement, *swiftly* there was movement. Eddie's virtual stomach nearly emptied itself. Everything reeled dizzily, dementedly into reverse, himself and Bex excepted. The virtual reality chamber blurred into the Spy High corridors into the rec room into the corridors into the study elevator into the upper school and Eddie realised what was happening, they were following Rose's memories backwards and now they were driving away from the college and Rose had yet to see it. But they still weren't travelling through time quickly enough to suit Jonathan Deveraux. 'Be prepared,' the founder warned. 'I am increasing the Mindwinder's speed to full velocity.'

And now Eddie had to clutch at Bex for support, physical rather than moral, as colours and sounds swirled crazily around them. But that was okay. Bex could hardly keep her balance either. 'I'm glad we haven't got to go back to her childhood!' he called out.

They started to slow. Eddie glimpsed himself pressing Rose down on to the courtyard of Knight's mansion, heard her sucking screams back into her lungs, saw them decide they'd better run inside again and that backwards was the way to do it. Getting close now. Deveraux temporarily reaccelerated the process. A shadow of the cells and then they were in realms of Rose's life to which he had not been witness. The sky loomed endless and dark above them, like a deep ocean in which you would certainly drown, overpowering and absolute, and it shocked Eddie to learn that this was how Rose regarded a simple natural phenomenon to which he'd never given a second thought.

Deveraux reduced their pace again. They were on a moor. A ridge in the distance was speckled with distinctive boulders but generally the site was barren and bare, save for a rather large and altogether artificial gash in the foreground. Here the soil had opened up and concrete doors concealing mysterious depths could be seen. Eddie knew what they meant. Beyond them, beneath them, lay the Pendragon Project.

He and Bex were not the only interested parties. Armed men stood in surly groups talking in nonsense. A helicopter's rotor-blades were circling anti-clockwise. Then he spied Rose. She was doubled up on the stony soil swallowing vomit in copious amounts, the sky crashing blackly over her head.

For a moment, Deveraux allowed the memory to play as it had weeks ago.

'Disgusting! . . . Weirdo . . . Better off leaving her here . . .' Knight's thugs' reaction to Rose was not favourable.

'Please, take me back!' Rose was pleading, begging, crawling, flinching from the sky as if it might leap at her at any second. Her hair and eyes were wild. Her grey overalls were stained with sick. 'I want my father! Please, let me see my father!'

She grabbed one of the men's legs desperately. He kicked her away.

'Looks like you're in there, mate.' Guffaws from the amused goons.

'Please, help me.' Rose sobbing. 'Somebody help me.'

'Rose . . .' Eddie was on the point of reaching out to her.

'You can't, Eddie.' Bex touched his shoulder. 'There's nothing you can do. She can't see or hear you. You weren't there.'

'So I've just got to watch? That's not good enough!' Eddie's eyes flashed in impotent fury. 'Hold on, though.' The thug who'd kicked out at Rose began to seem familiar.

He'd been at the mansion when Eddie had liberated Rose. The last he'd seen of him, the man hadn't exactly looked well. That was something, he supposed. 'Just you wait, big guy,' he promised darkly. 'You're going to get what's coming to you.'

The victim of Eddie's future violence didn't seem to care. He seized Rose's wrist like the wishbone of a turkey, yanked her across the ground towards the helicopter. 'Now are you gonna behave like a good girl or are we gonna have to *make* you behave?' His eyes gleamed at the prospect of the latter.

And Rose struggled like a fish on a line.

'Okay, okay!' Bex burst out. 'We've got a match by now, haven't we? Do we have to force Rose to relive all this trauma again? Dad?'

'You mean Rose can *feel* this memory as if it was actually happening now?' Eddie was dismayed. The Mindwinder was a torture machine.

'Dad?' Bex yelled stridently. 'Can you hear me?'

Either no, or yes but was ignoring her. Then one of Knight's men twisted an innocent-looking rock that happened to be lying there and the moor closed up to conceal the concrete doors, turfed them over and took them away.

'Dad, any chance we can stop now?'

'Agent Nelligan, Agent Deveraux,' came her father's voice, emotionless, 'the mindwind is over.'

There was just time for a final drink in the rec room before Eddie had to depart again for England. Bex seemed pensive, distant.

'A dollar for them?' Eddie offered. 'You know, what with inflation and everything.'

'Oh, they're not worth that,' Bex smiled wanly. 'Just, you know, thinking about the Mindwinder. It's what you said before: it worked – we've managed to find the project's location, moor and all, so your mission's still hot, and we all came out of the experience without even a bruise . . .'

'Is that the same as saying no one was hurt?'

'Was Rose hurt, having one of the most terrible moments of her life inflicted on her again?' Bex fiddled with her lip stud. 'I don't know, Ed, I just feel that sometimes these days, Dad gets his priorities wrong. He puts the assignment before the agent, the ends before the means. I mean, I know what we do carries risks, I know to an extent we're all expendable, when one of us doesn't make it Spy High's already got another agent trained to take our place – look at me and Jennifer – but I'd like to think that we still value each other in this organisation, that we value humanity. What are we supposed to be doing? Keeping the world safe for tomorrow. I want it to be a *human* tomorrow.'

'I'll drink to that,' said Eddie, downing the remainder of his Coke in one, 'and now I guess I'd better go. Bex, it's been a blast.'

'It's been like old times,' she concurred. 'Look after Rose, won't you, Eddie. She's going to need you, and people needing people, that's what it's all about.'

'I'd drink to that too, only I'm empty.' He leaned across instead and kissed her. 'Take care of yourself.'

Bex huffed, but good-humouredly. 'Take care of yourself too, Eddie. This Bartholomew Knight sounds like a dangerous guy and you're going to be on your own in the

Pendragon Project. Don't take any unnecessary chances.'

'Unnecessary chances?' Eddie scoffed. 'What, do I look like an idiot to you?'

But for some reason, Bex declined to answer.

NINE

Eddie reflected on Bex's words as he, Rose and Bowler flew east across the Atlantic on a private Deveraux jet. Her tone had been light, true, with no suggestion that he should have been making notes (unnecessary chances – avoid), but he still found himself wondering whether she'd have taken quite as much time to remind a former team-mate of the dangers involved in the field had the team-mate in question been Ben or Lori or Jake. Or Cally. Or anyone but himself, to be brutal. He still felt that on anybody's list of those Bond Teamers most likely to be around to draw their pension, he'd be sixth out of six, or maybe even seventh. So it was down to him to complete the mission successfully, as Agent Nelligan, not as the one in Bond Team who never got the girl and who only ever seemed to be there for comic relief. It was his responsibility to prove Bex's concerns misplaced, in the nicest possible way, of course.

She was already wrong about one thing. He wasn't going to be venturing inside the Pendragon Project alone; he was going to have a guide. He glanced across to

the other side of the table where Rose was playing soli-
taire and steadfastly refusing to lighten the glass of her
window so that she could see out. Mr Deveraux had
decided in his computerised wisdom that Rose Warwick
should accompany Agent Nelligan on the mission.
Firstly, infiltration by a spy was deemed preferable to
any kind of frontal assault on the project by a larger
body of men and women, at least until intelligence was
clearer as to the present disposition of those within.
Secondly, while Rose's memories of her home had
enabled the techs to extrapolate a complete model of the
facility to help Eddie find his way around once entry had
been secured, it was considered that the presence of
someone personally familiar with the project's lay-out
might still be useful. And thirdly, Eddie might well have
need of allies if Knight and his minions were, as seemed
probable, making the complex their base of operations:
what better way to win Henry Warwick to the Deveraux
side than to return to him his daughter?

He just had to hope she was ready for such an under-
taking.

'You all right, Rose?' Eddie asked cautiously.

'I think so.' She looked up from her game. 'I will be.
You won't have to worry about me, Eddie.'

'I probably shouldn't be saying this, Rose, but just
between you and me, if you really don't feel up to
coming with me on this mission, say so before it's too
late. Nobody could be surprised, given what you've
already been through.' Including the Mindwinder, he
thought. 'Nobody would think any the worse of you.'

Rose's green eyes narrowed. 'Don't you want me with
you, Eddie?'

'Of course I do,' he protested. 'I just don't want you getting hurt. I want to make sure you know the risks involved.'

'Eddie,' she reached for his hand across the table, 'I'd do anything to see my father again, take any risk. You're giving me a chance to go home and I'm not going to let that pass or let you down. I'm learning all the time, aren't I?' She smiled. 'A few days ago I could hardly bear to look at the sky. Now I'm up in it, flying through it, like the birds we used to watch on film in the Stone Garden.' She turned her gaze nervously to the darkened window. 'I know I've still got a long way to go before I'm what you surface people would call normal, Eddie . . .'

'Hey Rose, I've never been big on normal. Normal is as normal does. Variety is the spice of life, etc.'

'Yes, well.' Rose regarded him levelly, seriously. 'I'm just saying, I'm coming with you, Eddie, and you can rely on me. I promise.'

'Ditto,' said Eddie. He realised they were still squeezing hands. It kind of felt like one of those lean gently forward and kiss her kind of moments. He wondered if she'd *ever* been kissed before. Would he be the first?

Not right now, anyway. With a sense of timing matched only by the iceberg with the Titanic, Bowler strode down the cabin towards them. 'We shall be landing soon, Master Edward, Miss Rose,' he said. 'It might be sensible to put your seatbelts on again. We don't want any accidents, do we?'

'No, Bowler,' sighed Eddie, 'we sure don't.'

But the liaison man needn't have worried. The operation continued to proceed fluently and without a hitch. They landed exactly on time and were immediately transferred from private jet to what looked like a normal haulage company's wheelless truck but wasn't. Certainly, the foodstuffs that were brightly advertised on the truck's side had never been anywhere near the interior; the load that the vehicle *did* carry was not for the eyes of the general public. Once they were settled in their seats, Bowler gave the order for the drive northwards to begin. There was a particular patch of moorland they had an interest in up country.

As soon as the Mindwinder's images had allowed the location of the Pendragon Project to be pinpointed, Deveraux spy satellites had been turning their beady and almost infinitely magnifiable eyes on the site. A number of innocent-looking hikers had pitched their tents at exactly the spot where, weeks earlier, Bartholomew Knight's helicopter had awaited a reluctant passenger torn from the bowels of the earth. Hikers who seemed to spend a lot of their time strolling up and down over precisely that area of thin grass and soil that Rose's memories had revealed marked the hidden entrance to the Pendragon Project. Coincidence? It was not for spy satellites to speculate, but when their human masters identified the weapons in the apparent hikers' clothes, it didn't seem likely. Matching their faces against the Spy High database they found that almost all had been in the rec room at Little England during Eddie's visit there.

So entering through the front door wasn't an option. Agent Nelligan was going to have to burrow his way in. Hence the wheelless truck and its contents.

They parked a safe distance from the project, where Knight's men couldn't possibly see them. The techs unloaded and prepared the terraprobe while Eddie and Rose looked on.

'Just a final reminder, Master Edward,' intruded Bowler politely.

'Wrap up warm and take an umbrella?' Eddie and Rose had both changed into regulation shocksuits, with Eddie also fully equipped with sleepshot and shock blaster. This time he was entering the villain's lair without even a hint of Admiral Nelson.

'Your mission's parameters once more,' Bowler said, 'which strangely do not seem to include making flippant remarks at every available opportunity.'

'Sorry, Bowler,' Eddie said. So even Mr Dignity could crack a little from time to time. 'Please.'

'You are to establish the present situation within the Pendragon Project,' Bowler said. 'You are to seek support among the scientist community. You are to determine the nature of Mr Bartholomew Knight's plans and the extent to which they have progressed. You have license to disrupt these plans if possible but without —'

'I know,' Eddie winced. 'Without taking unnecessary chances.'

'Indeed, Master Edward.' Bowler sounded pleased to hear it. 'And, as always, you have a communicator in your belt. One would be delighted if you were to use it.'

'Bowler,' winked Eddie, 'get a chance and I'll send you a postcard.'

Bowler sighed faintly, looked beyond Eddie and Rose. 'Master Edward, Miss Rose,' he announced, 'your transport awaits.'

The terraprobe appeared something like a two-person bobsleigh, though to its basic chassis had been added several uncustomary design features, equipping it for burrowing beneath the earth rather than hurtling down a track of ice. A magnetic core was built into its nose, which then tapered to a glittering and powerful diamond drill bit. Its metal flanks were less streamlined than most Deveraux vehicles, thicker in order to accommodate the chutes through which debris would pass to be disgorged from the rear of the machine as it dug its way underground like a silver mole. Its passengers would be protected from suffocation by a reinforced transparent bubble that could be activated to secure them within a safe and self-sustaining atmosphere. What with Sky-Bikes, AquaBikes and now terraprobes, Deveraux transportation had the elements pretty well sewn up, Eddie thought.

'After you,' he said to Rose, who lowered herself into the rear seat as if she was stepping into a hot bath. 'Bowler, we'll be in touch. Don't go too far. Though I do recommend you step back a little in a moment or two.'

Eddie strapped into his own seat and checked that all systems were online. 'Activating air bubble,' he said, keying the relevant command into the control panel. 'See you, Bowler.'

'Good fortune, Master Edward, Miss Rose.'

Bowler moved away as the curved shield rose from the left side of the terraprobe, enveloped both passengers, and clicked into place beneath the chassis on the right. Yellow light automatically flooded the now sealed compartment – Eddie and Rose wouldn't be able to trust to sunlight for very much longer. Eddie booted up the magnetic core. The probe rose on hydraulic legs, tipped forward as the drill bit whirred.

Rose squealed as it made its first juddering contact with the earth, and the probe's front end sank into the churning soil. Entry was made. Eddie eased the machine towards acceleration. A final glance to the side and he saw Bowler on his communicator, no doubt informing Mr Deveraux that the mission was underway.

Then the surface vanished, along with the moor and the sky and everything but the earth's black and stony innards.

'You okay, Rose?' Luckily, the interior compartment was soundproofed, so conversation was eminently possible above the reduced whine of the frantic drill bit.

'I'm fine, Eddie.' Emphatically. 'Remember, I'm used to living with millions of tons of mud and rock above my head.' The drill sparked like electricity as it encountered a swathe of the latter. 'Can the probe manage?'

'Oh, sure.' Equally as emphatically. 'The bit on this baby could take us all the way to the centre of the earth if we wanted it to.'

'We don't, though, do we?'

'I've got a feeling our reception could be more than hot enough where we're going,' grinned Eddie, 'and don't worry, the Deveraux satellites have taken readings of the Pendragon Project site. We know its dimensions and where its outer walls are. Our course has been plotted and programmed into the terraprobe's navigation system. All you need to do is sit back and enjoy the ride.'

'I think I have something in common with Mr Bowler,' Rose said. 'Sometimes, Eddie, I'm not sure I understand your sense of humour. How am I supposed to sit back and enjoy anything while my father could be in danger of his life, my home at the mercy of Bartholomew Knight? How can you make jokes at times like this?'

'Believe me,' said Eddie, 'it's not easy. But if I didn't –' he turned in his seat to look at Rose – 'I think I'd have been a screaming wreck long ago. It's the pressure, Rose. Every mission, every day can be life or death. You learn to cope, that's part of our training at Spy High, and if you weren't prepared for a bit of stress in the first place you'd have been better off going to librarian school, but it's relentless and exhausting and it's hard. Everyone copes in their own way. Mine, I'm afraid –' he shrugged – 'is the one-liners. I don't know what else to do.'

'Look out!' came an idea from Rose.

Eddie snapped round just in time to see the earth crumble away ahead of them and the terraprobe's lights peer out across what seemed to be a black precipice. He quickly switched to flight mode as the machine plunged into empty space.

'Eddie!' gasped Rose, more in wonderment than fear.

He could see why. Precipice had been a little melodramatic. The probe had emerged into a colossal and man-made cavern deep underground, curved to accommodate the huge, blank-walled metal construction that dominated it like a World War II bunker of extraordinary proportions. Eddie joined his companion in exhalations of awe as he guided their machine between iron girders thicker than redwood trees that extended at intervals from the central structure and embedded themselves into sheets of surrounding rock, almost like mighty metal arms keeping the earth at a distance. The vast edifice may not have borne an identifying name on its impregnable flanks, but both Eddie and Rose knew what it was. Their journey had reached its end. The Pendragon Project lay before them.

'We've got to get in! How do we get in?' Rose was almost panting with her excitement.

'Don't panic, don't panic,' Eddie steered the terraprobe low, to the base of the complex, played the light along its rim. 'The techs said there'd have to be exterior access to maintenance areas for use during construction. In other words,' he pointed triumphantly ahead, 'a door.'

He landed the vehicle in the chasm between earth and project. Now Rose too could distinguish a door in the metal. She bit her lip in feverish anxiety. On the other side she would at last be reunited with her father. So why wasn't Eddie unfurling the bubble? 'Just letting Bowler know where we are,' he supplied. 'Put your belt-breather on, Rose. Until we get inside the air's not going to be too sweet.'

While Eddie communicated with the surface, Rose did as she was told, removing from her shocksuit's belt an item similar to a boxer's gum-shield and fitting it into her mouth. The belt-breather, Mr Bowler had informed her, provided a ten minute supply of oxygen for an agent's use under emergency circumstances. It wasn't the strangest thing she'd heard since Bartholomew Knight had arrived to change her life for ever.

'Okay? Let me check,' said Eddie, switching off the communicator.

'Uh uh uh *uhuh*,' complained Rose.

'I know you're not a baby,' said Eddie. 'Or was that I think I love you?' A slap suggested the former, and maybe also some increased understanding of Eddie's coping mechanisms. 'Okay, just follow exactly what I do. We'll be in before you know it.'

Rose hoped so. As Eddie disengaged the shielding and exposed them both to the atmosphere this far underground, she realised why they both needed the belt-breathers. The stench of dark soil alone made her want to gag, the reek of putrefaction. It was like being alive in a grave. Her skin crawled and her stomach heaved.

Eddie was working quickly at the door, with concentration and purpose. He could do it when he wanted to, she realised, or when he *had* to. But the silence was as heavy on her as the earth above. Even if she didn't always appreciate them, she missed his jokes. He was finishing at the door, had applied some putty-like materials to its rusted locks. Rose didn't need him to signal her to stand back. Given her father's line of work, she recognised plastic explosive when she saw it.

Eddie waded through mud to her, sheltered her body with his own. The detonation was dulled and deadened by lack of air, but the intent hadn't been to make a noise.

The door flapped open. Fresher air gusted out. The way was clear.

Rose took Eddie's hand, locked her eyes to his. There was gratitude in her expression. He'd brought her home and she'd never forget it. The doorway beckoned. Unafraid now, she led him towards the inner recesses of the Pendragon Project.

Eddie wasn't sure exactly what he expected to find in the complex. But it was a little disappointing that the maintenance level at least resembled just about every other kind of scientific or industrial installation he'd infiltrated during his time at Spy High. There were the same ducts and monitors and instruments, only maybe here on a smaller budget, and the same hum in the air. And there was the same last chance to take stock before the mission really began.

'I don't think we need these any more,' he said, replacing his belt-breather at his waist. 'But I *do* think we'd benefit from a bit of advance warning.' Eddie pressed a stud on his belt. Blue light spilled forth like water from a tap before resolving itself into a three-dimensional image of the Pendragon Project, complete with handy flashing red light for You Are Here. 'We are there,' Eddie pointed out for Rose's illumination, 'and your dad's living-booth is over here, which means all we have to do—'

'No, Eddie.'

'Huh? I haven't even said yet.'

Rose didn't care. 'You were *going* to say all we have to do is make our way to the home level and wait for dad in his living-booth. That's not a good idea. We'd have to pass through some of the busiest areas of the project. It'll increase our chances of being seen.'

'You reckon?' Eddie considered. Insider knowledge was, after all, one of the reasons Rose was there. 'Okay, so what are our alternatives?'

'The Stone Garden.' Rose dabbed at it with her finger. The blue room trembled like a cobweb. 'It's on a lower level so it's nearer to us and virtually nobody goes there these days.' She grinned at Eddie. 'Except my father.'

'I like the way you think,' Eddie grinned back. 'Rose Warwick, this could be the beginning of a beautiful partnership. Let's switch to radar visors and we'll be ready.'

The two teenagers pulled thin strips of what seemed to be plastic film from their belts and wrapped them around their eyes. Where the film's ends met at the back of their heads there was the faintest click, securing the visor in place. 'I'm seeing the circle,' said Eddie. Three hundred and sixty-five degree vision guaranteed. In the spy game it was as important to know what lurked behind you as what lay ahead. Radar vision also threw in right and left and through walls for good measure.

'Keep close to me, Rose,' Eddie counselled. There hadn't been time for her to do a lot of training with the visors, but her lips were set in fierce concentration. She was going to be all right.

They moved off, spurning the elevators (too enclosed) and keeping instead to the stairwells. Up a level to storage and food production, still nowhere you'd expect to encounter crowds. Up again to more public spaces – the recreation level. The complex was beginning to depress Eddie. It was all so grey and cramped and narrow, like all the life and colour and joy had been sapped from it years ago, leaving only a rusting shell behind. It was as if he'd stepped into a black and white movie, curling at the corners, from a time and a place long past. He couldn't wait to get to the final reel. And to think, the worst of it was, Rose had been *born* here, raised here. This place was her life, her only home. She *liked* it. While Eddie was already feeling the dismal walls closing in on him and claustrophobia beckoning from the back of his mind, he could see that Rose was perfectly comfortable, gazing about her with the pleasure of greeting old friends. At least she'd now had experience of the surface world, the *real* world of 2066, Eddie just hoped she'd see that her future lay there. Maybe that was the one good thing Bartholomew Knight had done during this whole affair, however unintentionally, opened Rose's eyes to the truth of what was around her. Eddie would remember to thank him before they shipped him off to his cell.

But he was allowing his mind to wander. Bowler would not approve. A spy's mind in the field should be kept like a dog on a walk, securely on a leash. He had to focus. The Stone Garden was close.

But so were people.

'Back!' he hissed to Rose, forewarned by radar vision. He tugged her down with him into the shadows of a doorway as a man and a woman came their way. Scientists, he thought, project natives. They were wearing the same shapeless, colourless overalls that he'd first seen on Rose. They looked about sixty but they could have been younger, prematurely aged by their unhealthy and sunless existence underground. The man wore steel-rimmed spectacles that Eddie doubted had been in fashion for hundreds of years. The skin of both of them was not so much pale as *grey*, as if dust had settled into their pores and was breeding there.

Rose squeezed his shoulder. 'That's Professor Syme and his wife,' she whispered excitedly, like she'd just spotted a celebrity. 'They're good people. They'll help us.'

'Not yet.' Eddie cautioned her. Now wasn't the time to give their presence away. 'Your father first.'

Reluctantly, Rose nodded. It was as well she did.

'Professor Syme!' A cold, sneering voice. Two more newcomers, both male, both armed, the speaker

Frankie Garvey. 'Mr Knight wants to see you in the test lab.'

'We're on our way there now,' said Professor Syme, with a lofty contempt in his tone that suggested Rose could be right.

'I'm pleased to hear it,' snorted Garvey, 'though most people would probably go *this* way.' The opposite direction to that taken by the Symes. 'How about if Rennard and I accompany you, Professor? We wouldn't want you getting lost now, would we?'

Eddie watched as the scientists were marched away. Part of him had almost hoped that Frankie Garvey would notice him and Rose crouched there, give him an excuse to shoot the shaven-haired moron. But it wasn't to be. That was a pleasure that would have to wait. The mission came first.

'They're still here then,' Rose said bitterly. 'Bartholomew Knight is still in control.'

'Looks like it,' Eddie acknowledged. 'For now.'

'The things he could have done.' Rose didn't seem to want to specify them. 'Let's find my father.'

'What is the Stone Garden anyway?'

'It's a place of reflection,' Rose described, 'a place to go to be peaceful and calm and quiet. The Memory Wall is there, where we commemorate those patriotic scientists who have died here It's where their ashes are kept, where my mother's ashes are kept, close to the last reminders of the world our ancestors left behind.'

Eddie saw what she meant. He wouldn't exactly have used the word *garden*. Garden to him meant flowers and growth and *green* rather than grey. Stone, though, he could see where that was coming from. An arched vault including space to stroll and places to sit and watch any of the dozen or more screens – Eddie recognised them as old-fashioned televisions – that showed film not only of the natural world confined to the surface far above, but also of a society and a technology that was even harder to reach. Obsolete petrol-driven cars, men and women in antique fashions making inexplicable gyrations to the gramophone, cityscapes that hadn't existed in those forms for decades, smiles on faces long in the grave. The 1950s captured on camera for a scientist population imprisoned in the past. Eddie didn't doubt that there was plenty of scope for reflection in the Stone Garden, but none of it he imagined would be conducive to peacefulness or calm. In time it would have had him screaming. No wonder the place was deserted.

Except for one man.

His back was to them and he was touching the tips of his fingers against an inscription carved on what was clearly the Memory Wall. Rose didn't need to see his face. Eddie couldn't have stopped her crying out and running to him even if he'd tried.

She tore off her radar visor. 'Father!' she cried.

'Rose? Rose!' The man turned and Eddie saw him. He could have been Professor Syme. The Pendragon Project reduced everyone to the same shrunken grey shadow. But not Rose. He wasn't going to let that happen to Rose.

He watched father and daughter embrace in tears and was pleased for both of them. Yet the Memory Wall was in his sight as well, no doubt with a little room for Rose's ashes reserved. Well, in her case the wall was going to be disappointed. When all this was over, he was going to take Rose Warwick away from this high-tech tomb. Whether she liked it or not.

Eddie realised that in somewhere like the Pendragon Project space was always going to be at a premium, but he thought the complex's original architects might have given their Head Scientist slightly larger quarters. Living-*booth* was right. There wasn't room to swing a kitten in here. Just a desk, chair, wardrobe and bed. Father and daughter were hugging each other on the latter, Warwick holding on to Rose as if she might vanish again as soon as he let her go.

'My pretty Rose, my prettiest Rose in England,' he crooned, 'back with me again.'

'Yeah, yeah.' Eddie tried to master his impatience. 'I know this is a moving family reunion and everything, I appreciate that, but I've got a job to do here and lives may depend on it. *Please*, Professor Warwick, can we talk about Knight?'

'Eddie,' Rose scolded. 'Everything's going to be all right now. Don't worry.'

'No, perhaps your young friend is right, Rose,' conceded Warwick warily, blinking at Eddie through thick spectacles, 'though let me point out to you, Agent Nelligan, that simply because I no longer have faith in Bartholomew Knight, that does *not* mean that I automatically trust you and your organisation. It has not escaped my attention that you have both used my daughter to influence me, Knight stealing her away and you bringing her back.'

'No, Dad, it's not like that,' Rose pleaded with him. 'You can trust Eddie. *I* trust him.'

'It seems you've made quite an impression on my daughter, Agent Nelligan,' observed Henry Warwick, 'so I'll give you the benefit of the doubt, even though in the society in which the project has its roots, the idea of teenage secret agents would have been preposterous.'

'It doesn't always make a lot of sense now,' said Eddie, 'but plenty's changed since this place was sealed, Professor Warwick. Not all of it's good, but not everyone's like Bartholomew Knight.'

'I'm pleased to hear that,' sighed Henry Warwick, 'and perhaps one day now, I'll see the surface world for myself, see the England my grandparents left behind a hundred years ago. I'd like to feel the sun on my skin once before I die.'

'Don't talk about dying, Father,' Rose said.

'Bartholomew Knight?' Eddie prompted.

'He's been here for days now, plundering our weaponry. I imagine you're secretly critical, Agent Nelligan, whether you say so or not. Critical that we of the project should place such potentially devastating tools in the hands of a man so palpably unfit to possess them.' Eddie suspected here was his cue to vigorously deny that any such thought had crossed his mind. He couldn't do it. 'But you must first understand the principles that have underpinned our existence in this place for so long. Since the Pendragon Project was sealed, our work has been everything, our inspiration and our reason for living. Our grandparents entered here willingly, knowing that under the Project Charter they were subordinating their individual lives to our great cause, to the future welfare of our country. They died gladly beneath the ground. Our parents followed them, my wife, too, Rose's mother. And throughout the years of our voluntary exile, we have been taught that whichever man of the surface finally makes contact with us, we must obey him immediately and absolutely as the rightful representative of Britain.'

'So you just accepted what Knight said?' Eddie struggled to believe that such abject gullibility could coexist with Warwick's obvious supreme scientific intellect. 'You didn't ask questions?'

'We were not born to ask questions of those from the surface,' Warwick said. 'But now, when daily I see the kind of man Bartholomew Knight is, when Rose is taken from me and my old certainties with her, now I begin to ask questions, and I very much fear the answers. Has my life's work been wasted? Have my priorities been wrong all this time? What have I done?'

'It's not your fault, Father.' Rose stroked his brow delicately. 'You did what you were born to do.'

'Everyone has a choice, darling Rose,' said Warwick. 'It's what makes us human.'

'Well now you can choose to help kick Knights' ass,' urged Eddie. 'So to speak.'

Professor Warwick smiled wearily but shook his head. 'It cannot be my decision alone,' he said. 'I am Head Scientist, but on matters of project policy the Group Heads collectively must reach agreement.'

Rules, Eddie cursed inwardly. Procedures. Conventions. Scientists fiddling while Britain burned. 'Can we kind of ask them, then?'

'They are coming,' said Warwick, 'but they must not be seen together. Bartholomew Knight frowns on social gatherings of any kind. He says they are unpatriotic. We must wait.'

Fortunately for Eddie's nerves, it wasn't for long. Three other men and a woman finally crammed into the living-booth as if in preparation for an assault on one of those world records involving lots of people and an enclosed space. He recognised Professor Syme. The others were Professors Smith and O'Brien (the woman) and Dr Parsons. They were all entirely interchangeable, regardless of gender, but, Eddie quickly realised with a sinking heart, their opinions concerning what ought to be done about Bartholomew Knight were far from unified.

Syme he could rely on. He hugged Rose delightedly, listened to Eddie attentively, and was 'entirely clear' in his own mind that, whatever the man said to the contrary, Knight was 'an enemy of Britain, an enemy of freedom, and an enemy of ours'. Smith and O'Brien, on the other hand, were implacably opposed to any action against the surface-dwellers. 'Mr Knight came to us,' they argued. 'He knew how and where to find us. His advent is therefore the fulfilment of our purpose here and we owe him our loyalty. It is not for us to question the politics or the personalities of a world we have never seen.' Dr Parsons remained thoughtfully silent.

'Whatever conclusion we reach,' said Henry Warwick, 'on a matter of such gravity, a matter that could change the very nature of our existence here for ever, we must be unanimous.'

'We must be prompt, Henry,' remarked Syme, 'or it won't matter what we decide.'

'What do you mean, Professor Syme?' Eddie frowned.

'I mean that at the speed with which Knight is currently manufacturing the Pendragon Virus, it can't be long before he has all he could possibly need – I was with him in the test lab this afternoon. I am certain he will soon leave here to use it.'

'I know I'm not going to like the answer,' Eddie said worriedly, 'but could anybody let me know what the Pendragon Virus is?'

'A plague. An infection. A disease,' obliged Syme. 'It'll make the Black Death look like an outbreak of the common cold. Let loose in major population centres . . .' Syme shook his head. 'The cities will turn to graves.'

'Bio-weaponry is in the end so much more cost-effective than conventional munitions,' admired Professor Smith.

'The Pendragon Virus, Henry. Your greatest achievement,' praised Professor O'Brien.

'You created it?' Eddie turned to Rose's father eagerly. 'Then you'll know how it can be cured. You know how we'll be able to stop it.' He was thinking of the Europa Conference, the Millenium Halls littered with the bodies of dead delegates, their lungs clogged and corrupted with the Pendragon Virus. He was thinking that Bartholomew Knight would regard such an atrocity as a good start. What was he fond of saying? 'Our enemies are all around us'? They'd be fewer in number if he could spray them with virus. It couldn't be allowed to come to that.

But Henry Warwick gazed long and hard at Eddie, his expression blank.

'Father?' said Rose, almost fearfully.

'There is no anti-body,' said the Professor. 'That is the point. Once unleashed, the Pendragon Virus cannot be stopped.'

TEN

'**O**kay,' said Eddie, 'so that's not exactly the best news I've had this week.' He figured he'd better start taking advantage of his licence to disrupt Bartholomew Knight's plans before they were past disruption. It would do no good to signal for an assault by Deveraux forces: as soon as he saw them coming Knight might just consider letting the virus stretch its deadly legs. No, Eddie had better see about closing down production himself.

'The Pendragon Virus was developed only as a defensive measure and as a last resort.' Henry Warwick seemed to be defending himself, though without a great deal of conviction. 'It was intended to protect this country against its enemies. Every single weapon that was ever invented in this complex shared that same, noble aim – to protect us. But now,' he hung his head in a defeated pose that seemed to be becoming habitual, 'how do we know who our enemies *are*?'

'We don't *have* to know, Henry.' Professor Smith. 'We only have to follow orders.'

'No, Dad.' Rose protested. 'Knight threatened me. Eddie helped me. You have to help him.'

O'Brien pitched in, quoting the Project Charter. Syme added his voice, questioning whether a document written a hundred years ago could have any validity now. Eddie felt his head whirling.

'Hold it. Hold it!' A pause. 'Listen, you guys can talk all you want, and argue and split hairs and do nothing. That's not an option for me. I need to see this test lab, wherever it is you say Knight's manufacturing the virus, and I'd quite like to see it before my next birthday. Now I could find my own way there, but it'd speed things along if one of you came with me. Any volunteers?'

'But we have yet to decide whether we support your organisation or not, lad,' said Professor Smith, annoyed at being rushed.

'I'll take you.' Eddie started. He'd almost forgotten Dr Parsons was in the room. 'I have access authority to enter the test lab. I'll take you.'

'Dr Parsons, thank you.' Eddie prepared to leave. 'Rose —'

'I'll be all right, Eddie. I'll be safe with my father.'

'Okay, I won't be long.'

The reticent scientist led Eddie out of the living-booth and into the home level corridor. 'Remember, Doc,' whispered Eddie, 'I'm not sure I'm exactly Mr Popular with your colleagues but I am *sure* that I'm not going to be welcomed with open arms by Knight and his cronies. We find shadows and we stick to 'em.'

'I know what to do,' said Dr Parsons.

They ghosted their way to the experimentation and development level, having to take evasive manoeuvres only occasionally in order to keep out of sight of a guard. The atmosphere inside the project seemed to have dulled Knight's men's brains, not that they could ever have been described as intellectual giants, but they seemed bored, listless. Excellent, Eddie thought.

'The test lab,' Parsons at last indicated a laboratory beyond a windowed steel wall and door. Unoccupied. Another excellent. 'The viral strain is kept here.' He keyed his entry code into a control pad alongside the door. 'Quickly.'

They slipped inside and Parsons closed not only the door but metal shields against the window, protecting them from passing eyes. Reassured, Eddie turned his attention to the lab's contents: phials and jars of bubbling chemicals, oval capsules in black like the eyes of skulls, each marked with a serial number. 'Are these for carrying the virus?' Parsons confirmed that they were. Eddie wasn't sure he dared touch them. How many people could one small capsule of virus kill, a delicate glass container no bigger than an egg? Thousands? Hundreds of thousands? It was death to go, and Bartholomew Knight had placed one hell of an order.

Eddie unclipped his belt camera and took photographs of everything. The techs at Spy High weren't into holiday snaps, but they couldn't get enough of pictures of biological weapons. 'I guess this is one lab where butter fingers aren't welcome, you think, Doc? . . . Dr Parsons?'

Gone.

Eddie swore under his breath. Parsons had evidently evacuated, and without telling him. Why – on both counts? Whatever, it would probably be wise to follow suit.

But he'd left it too late. Eddie knew it as soon as the shields started to go up again. He wasn't surprised to see a number of Knight's men outside, all rather more alert now, all with pulse rifles at the ready. He wasn't surprised to see a grinning Frankie Garvey in their midst. He supposed he wasn't even surprised to see Dr Parsons rubbing rounded grey shoulders with them. He must have summoned them, after all.

'That shock blaster you're thinking of reaching for,' advised Garvey over the commlink, 'I wouldn't, Nelligan. Not where you're standing.' He shook his head in mock commiseration. 'Looks like I've beaten you yet again.'

'Agent Nelligan,' said Bartholomew Knight, with a smile as thin as a razor, 'we must stop meeting like this.'

Eddie had been transferred to a less volatile lab, but one that could be equally well locked and guarded. He had no control over his visitors. 'Frankly, Knight,' he said, 'I'd sooner not meet you at all, but all the while you persist with your mad schemes and strange ideas of patriotism I guess it's gonna have to keep happening.'

'No,' said Knight, 'I think you'll find this is the last time.'

'What? You're gonna have Tower and Ben sit on me?' Eddie regarded Knight's personal bodyguards with something akin to amazement. It wasn't simply that the ceilings in the project were low. The two men really *were* nine feet tall, give or take an inch, and Eddie sensed that they hadn't stopped growing yet. They were having to stoop forward, their bodies bulging with the kind of musculature usually reserved for cartoon characters. Before long their knuckles would be trailing along the ground.

'Guess it's hard to find fashionable clothes in your sizes, huh?' The bodyguards were draped in what could once have been tents.

'Tower and Ben took part in a little experiment for me,' said Knight. 'They were injected with a course of growth hormones developed by Dr Parsons here. An army of unstoppable giant soldiers would be such an asset on the battlefield, don't you agree? The effects, as you can see, are really quite astounding. They even seem to be accelerating.'

'So no more smart remarks, kid,' slurred the Tower of London, as if his tongue was becoming too heavy to lift. He opened a massive fist. 'Or I'll squeeze your head in here and pop it like a zit.'

'That won't be necessary,' snapped Knight distaste-fully. 'Agent Nelligan's demise is going to be rather more helpful to our plans than that.'

'Don't tell me,' guessed Eddie. 'Trial run for the Pendragon Virus?'

Knight smiled again. 'I'd start practising holding your breath now.'

'I've had some experience. And let me guess, this is all so the bug is ready for when you infect everyone at the Europa Conference.'

'Nelligan,' lamented Knight, 'if you had only trained as a psychic instead of a secret agent, you might have lived longer.'

'Yeah, but would I have met such wonderful people?'

'A pity you won't be there to witness my final triumph,' Knight continued, 'as with one fell swoop Albion eradicates the corrupt and conniving leadership of Europa, including that gang of traitors masquerading as the British Government. But there you have it, Nelligan. You'll just have to content yourself with the knowledge that you will, in a small way, have played a part in the rebirth of England. Parsons, prepare the chamber.'

'Yes, sir,' grovelled Dr Parsons. 'But sir, if I may, my loyalty *will* be rewarded, will it not?'

Bartholomew Knight's eyes sparkled like black diamonds. 'I'll think of a suitable reward, Parsons. I promise you that. And now that you mention it, it might be time to remind one or two others of where their loyalties lie.'

When they came for Rose, Henry Warwick howled. In horror. In rage. In helplessness. 'Not again!' he cried. 'You mustn't take her again!'

'Mr Knight's orders, sir,' sneered Frankie Garvey, shoving the scientist away. 'But don't worry. Nothing bad's gonna happen to her. So long as you do as you're told.'

Professor Syme, to his credit, made a feeble lunge at Garvey. His glasses were smashed by the butt of the terrorist's pulse rifle. They were on his nose at the time. There was blood.

Rose did not protest as the nightmare descended on her again. She knew from experience that to do so would not help her at all. Only Eddie could do that. She needed Eddie.

And neither Garvey nor any of his companions bothered to look behind them at Henry Warwick, kneeling by the side of the groaning Professor Syme. It might have been worth their while to have glanced back. Bartholomew Knight might have been interested to hear of the new expression on the Head Scientist's face. The crazed, desperate expression of the man pushed, if not yet over the edge, then to its very limit.

At least Knight hadn't thought it necessary to keep Eddie and Rose apart. One makeshift cell was apparently easier to guard than two.

'What are we going to do? I'm scared they'll hurt my father. Can't we contact Mr Bowler for help?'

'Not without my communicator,' Eddie said, 'and even Garvey had enough sense to take my belt and anything that looked like a weapon. Including the sleepshot this time.'

'Then it's hopeless?'

'It's never that,' assured Eddie. He beckoned her closer, so that the guard on the lab door couldn't hear. 'These suits we're wearing have a certain property that our fanatical friends don't know about. There's not been a good opening to use it yet, too many of Knight's men around, but give me half a chance and I'll show you just why they're called shocksuits.'

'Don't stop there, Eddie,' taunted a familiar voice from the doorway. 'Give the girl a kiss. Lord knows you need the practice.'

Boudica. And Garvey. Eddie felt Rose squeezing his hand, a movement he returned encouragingly. Looked like their half a chance was on its way.

'I should have known you'd be round here somewhere, Boudica,' said Eddie. 'Either here or under a rock, it was a bit of a toss-up which. And hey, I hope you've recovered from the tumble you had hunting. It's such a downer when the fox bites back, isn't it?'

'Why, you . . .' Garvey jerked forward and lifted his pulse rifle as if to ram it down on Eddie's skull. Eddie braced himself.

'Don't fall for it, you idiot.' Boudica restrained her hot-tempered companion. 'He's only trying to rile us.'

'Yeah, you're right, Bou,' Garvey said, suitably chastened. 'Let him try.'

'Bou?' Eddie laughed. 'Bou? How come I never got to call you Bou? Does this mean the two of you are like an item, then? Frankie and Bou?'

'What we are, Eddie,' declared Boudica coldly, 'is no business of yours.'

'Yeah, but come on, Bou,' pursued Eddie, 'I know we kind of reached a parting of the ways, you know, when you tried to kill me, but I still feel sufficient residual warmth towards you to hope you'd do better than this jerk.'

'That's it!' Garvey flipped again. 'Say goodbye to those teeth!'

'No, Frankie.' And this time Boudica's voice held anger too. 'I don't care what you think, Eddie.'

'Ah,' Eddie waggled his finger, 'but I think you do. Otherwise, why bother to come visit? You could have just applauded me to the gas chamber.'

'I'm *gonna* applaud you to the gas chamber, Nelligan,' confirmed Frankie Garvey. 'I can't wait.'

'*You* wanted to see me first though, didn't you, Boudica?' Eddie persisted. One last push, he thought. He had to be right. Her eyes were darkening like storm clouds, her nostrils flaring. 'You wanted to see me with Rose. I think you're jealous.'

'Shut up, Eddie.'

'That's it, isn't it?' It surprised him how patently

obvious Boudica's feelings now were. 'You *are* jealous. What's the problem? Spoiled little rich girl used to having everything her own way? Sorry, Bou, but even if your dad wasn't a murderous lunatic, I'd choose Rose over you every time.'

'Shut up!'

Maddened, Boudica threw herself at Eddie. She should have listened to her own advice. Eddie was on his feet to meet her, keeping her between him and Garvey's pulse rifle. His fingers flashed beneath his cuff to boot up his shocksuit. It shimmered with current, crackled as Boudica collided with it, jolted her backwards with a cry of pain. Eddie was lashing out at Garvey before the terrorist could react, his fists landing with a satisfying crunch, the blow accompanied by a shower of electric sparks. As Garvey clattered to the floor, Eddie pivoted and kicked at the guard in the doorway. Fireworks exploded beneath the man's chin.

'Rose, come on!'

They burst out of the lab. Maybe to return to Henry Warwick. Maybe to the test lab. Maybe they were better off trying to make it back to the terraprobe . . .

Or maybe not.

Bartholomew Knight and rather too many lackeys for himself and Rose to out-fight packed the corridor. The shocksuit would probably only tickle Tower and Ben in any case.

'Going somewhere, Agent Nelligan?' said Knight curiously. 'I think not.'

An announcement went out over the commlink that all Pendragon Project personnel should gather in the Stone

Garden on the hour for a broadcast from Bartholomew Knight. When the time came, virtually all of the fifty or so scientists and their handful of children had indeed congregated there, were milling about and murmuring in confused groups, many casting inquiring glances in the direction of their leader, Professor Henry Warwick. There were two absences. Dr Parsons was one. Rose Warwick was the other.

'I want to see my daughter,' the Head Scientist demanded of one of the guards who encircled his people. 'I have to see her. Now. Tell Knight. Tell him.'

'I'm not telling Mr Knight nothing,' said the guard obstinately, 'and neither are you. Now step back with the others, Professor Warwick, there's a good boy, before I make you.' The man's pulse rifle glittered like a smile.

'Henry. Come away.' Syme plucked at his sleeve. 'It'll do you no good.'

'But . . . what's happened?' Warwick gazed around him as if seeing the project for the first time. 'What are we doing here?' The grey shuffles of scientists, like prisoners in a labour camp. The men with guns and hard, ugly faces. Screens mocking them all with televisual memories of a dead world. 'It's all gone wrong. Where's Rose? She's our only hope.'

'Quiet, Henry,' hissed Syme. The 1950s had suddenly vanished from the screens. Bartholomew Knight replaced them.

'As all of you have no doubt heard by now,' he began, 'our complex has been infiltrated by an intruder from the surface. Someone who does not share our common goal – the protection of our proud nation through strength. An enemy. This intruder, you need have no

fear, is now in my custody. Yet it has come to my attention that some of you may have been influenced by his
lies . . .'

Eddie stood with his hands bound several levels above
the Stone Garden, Rose beside him, Garvey, Tower, Ben
and an assortment of other underlings beside her, all
watching Knight make his broadcast to the people of the
project. Eddie almost had to admire the man's appearance of wounded innocence, of heartfelt grievance that
anybody could possibly believe the intruder's slanderous
suggestions that he, Bartholomew Knight, was a
madman and a terrorist, rather than a *patriot*.

Eddie's eye strayed beyond the speaker to a conical
lead chamber around which Dr Parsons was fussing. It
was scarcely big enough to contain a man, and it
reminded him of the Iron Maidens that had been so
popular in medieval torture chambers. In both cases
comfort was not a priority. You stepped inside this
chamber to die.

And it was being readied for him.

Rose's eyes were wide with dread and he sympathised.
There seemed precious little way out of this now. No
weapons. No shocksuit – he'd been forced to exchange it
for the Pendragon Project overalls. No allies to stage a
last minute rescue.

Dr Parsons selected a capsule of the virus from a steel
container like a sweet from a box of chocolates. He
placed it, lovingly and very carefully, in a slot in the
chamber.

'Eddie . . .' mourned Rose.

In the Stone Garden, Professor Henry Warwick was
no longer listening to Knight's self-justification. Words

could be true or words could be false. It was the *speaker* who mattered, the speaker you had to trust or disbelieve. And you learned the measure of a man by gazing into his eyes, by peering into his soul. Bartholomew Knight's eyes, the scientist realised, were black. There was no reason to suppose that his soul was any different.

'And so,' Knight was drawing to a close, 'I thought you would all benefit from a little demonstration of what happens to those foolish enough to stand against us.' He smiled an icicle smile at Eddie. 'Dr Parsons,' he said, 'be so good as to step inside the chamber, please.'

'What? Me? No!' For once, Dr Parsons was keen to make himself heard. 'What do you mean? You can't—'

'Oh, I can,' claimed Knight. 'I'd like Agent Nelligan to witness the effects of the Pendragon Virus on a man before he experiences them first-hand. It'll make his final moments of waiting all the more tense. The chamber, Parsons. Why aren't you in it?'

'But Mr Knight. *Sir*. I'm loyal.' It always pained Eddie to see a grown man beg, even one as odious as Parsons. 'I've done everything you've asked of me.'

'Not quite,' noted Knight. 'Tower.'

The giant bodyguard seized the scientist like a geriatric doll, thrust him screaming and writhing into the chamber. The door was secured. A monitor screen allowed those outside to observe a frantic Dr Parsons kicking and pounding futilely, giving his doomed lungs one final vocal burst of exercise.

'Watch closely, Nelligan,' recommended Bartholomew Knight. 'You're next.'

In the Stone Garden, too, all eyes were on the screens. Except Henry Warwick's. If Knight was happily prepared to kill Parsons, why would he baulk at removing anybody else if the whim took him? Syme, perhaps, or even himself. Or worse . . .

'Break the capsule,' ordered Knight.

Parsons knew it immediately. He ceased trying to escape the chamber. A lost and desolate wail rose in his throat. It was choked off halfway through. The invisible poison of the virus worked quickly. Parsons' eyes bulged. His jaw strained until it had to be off its hinges. His purpling tongue wriggled like a slug in the black pit of his mouth.

'The virus attacks the respiratory system, you see, Nelligan,' informed Knight conversationally. 'It corrodes most efficiently, wouldn't you say?'

Dr Parsons vomited a copious amount of blood. It was his final contribution to the world of the living.

'One down,' said Knight cheerily. 'One to go.'

But down in the Stone Garden, something inside Henry Warwick had snapped. A sense of duty, the certainties of a lifetime, a belief in his work or his place or the reason for his being, any or all of them were gone. Lost. There was only love for Rose now, and a burning hatred for the man who'd taken her away.

With a cry of inarticulate fury, a cry that was like a knife to the heart, Professor Henry Warwick attacked the nearest guard.

His shout wasn't heard up at the chamber, however, where the remains of Dr Parsons were being removed to make room for a second victim. Neither were the sounds of pulse rifles firing that followed.

'Agent Nelligan,' Knight was inviting, 'please. Or would you like Tower or Ben to assist you?'

'Assist me, I don't think so,' Eddie smiled thinly. 'Replace me, on the other hand . . .'

'Ah, witty until the end,' said Knight. 'How tiresome.'

Garvey was chuckling behind him and Eddie had to concede that maybe this time his old enemy had won after all. Boudica was looking at him too, but she was pale, not celebratory, and she turned away with a shudder. And Rose . . .

'Eddie, no!' She tried to hold him but they pulled her away. He'd never touch her again. He'd never touch anyone again.

'Be strong, Rose. Whatever happens. Stay strong.' He muttered under his breath: 'I'm not finished yet.'

But, as Eddie forced himself to take his first slow, faltering step towards the chamber, he feared it wouldn't be long.

ELEVEN

'Mr Knight! Sir!' One of the guards was suddenly racing towards them.

Eddie tensed. Any interruption was a good interruption, and the man sounded alarmed.

'Don't stop, Nelligan,' warned Knight.

'The scientists!' the hurtling guard cried.

'Father,' breathed Rose.

They glimpsed other figures behind the guard, multiple figures in grey. All armed. There was hesitation among Knight's men, their leader himself briefly uncertain what to do. And then it was obvious. When fired upon by pulse rifles, it was sensible to take cover.

The air erupted with pulse blasts and shock blasts, blistered with potential death. Knight's men returned fire and the chamber and Eddie's execution were forgotten, at least temporarily. Eddie fancied making it permanent. He slammed into the nearest guard, wielded his bound hands as a club and coshed the startled man to the floor.

Knight, meanwhile, had drawn his own shock blaster

and aimed at Rose, huddling against a wall, an easy target.

Eddie hurled the fallen guard's rifle at him. It struck Knight's arm, deflected his shot.

The scientists were gaining ground.

'We're leaving,' Knight announced. 'Now!'

'But, sir . . .' Frankie Garvey objected, particularly while Nelligan still had breath to draw.

'If a stray shot hits those capsules . . .' Knight didn't need to say more. 'Garvey, bring them. Fall back to the Seal. Do it!'

Garvey was going to obey, of course, but not before one final attempt on Eddie's life. He sprayed the corridor with pulse-blasts. Eddie dived as they riddled the wall behind him. Gasped as a sudden burning pain in his lower leg indicated that one shell at least had reached its target. But then Garvey was retreating with the rest and Rose's father and Professor Syme and twenty Pendragon scientists besides were surging around him.

Rose hugged Eddie fiercely. 'You're all right!'

'I am now.'

'No. You're not. You're hurt.' Her face showed shock at discovering his wound. 'You're bleeding.'

'It's nothing. A scratch. I just need a piece of material or something to bind it.'

'Father!' Rose transferred her affections. Warwick family reunions were getting to be a habit. 'Oh, I'm so glad to see you!'

'Rose isn't the only one,' said Eddie, tearing his trouser-leg to use as a makeshift bandage. 'If it wasn't for you, Professor Warwick, poor Doc Parsons over there would have had company. Thanks. But what happened? Group Heads finally made a decision?'

'*I* finally made a decision,' asserted Henry Warwick, his eyes steely with resolution now in a way they hadn't been before. 'I made a choice. To trust *you*, young man. To oppose Bartholomew Knight.'

'You should have seen your father, Rose,' said Professor Syme, incongruously carrying a pulse rifle and breathing hard from his exertions. 'He tackled an armed guard bare-handed, wrestled him to the floor. Another guard was going to shoot him but the rest of us weren't having that. The sight of Parsons' execution influenced even people like Smith and O'Brien. Knight's men had guns, but we had numbers. And a leader worth following.'

'Syme, it's too late,' dismissed Henry Warwick bitterly. 'I should have resisted Knight from the start. Whatever he claimed to be, it should have been obvious he was an evil man. But I allowed myself to be deceived, duped, exploited by stupid appeals to patriotism and loyalty, by the inertia of a lifetime wasted toiling blindly here beneath the ground. What does a country matter? It's people who matter.' He stroked his daughter's red hair tenderly. 'The people you love. And now, for my sins, I have given into a madman's hands a biological weapon with the power to murder millions. My name will be damned with Knight's and rightly so. It should be me lying there, not Parsons!'

'Father, don't,' comforted Rose.

'Rose is right, Professor Warwick.' Eddie stood gingerly, tested his weight on his injured leg. The muscles protested, but they'd just have to cope. 'We're not out of this yet. If we can prevent Knight from reaching the surface . . . He told his men to fall back to the Seal.'

'That's the only entrance to the complex,' said Henry Warwick. 'If they make it through there with the virus, we'll never be able to catch them.'

'Well, it's not quite the *only* entrance,' Eddie corrected. 'Professor, you and whoever's in fit condition to fight get after Knight and his men, put them under as much pressure as you can. Try to slow them down. Rose, try and find our belt communicator, let Bowler know it's time to move in.'

'What are you going to do, Eddie?'

With a wince he reached down for a fallen guard's shock blaster. 'I'm gonna try and give Bartholomew Knight a nasty surprise.'

He didn't relish the idea of retreat, there was something ignoble and unpatriotic about it. Bartholomew Knight's favourite military engagements of the past included the Charge of the Light Brigade and the Defence of Rorke's Drift, examples of reckless heroism and staunch, backs-against-the-wall last stands against incredible odds. His present flight from the Pendragon Project bearing several dozen capsules of viral death and being pursued by a motley collection of scientists firing guns did not have quite the same courageous ring to it. But then, it was a matter of priorities. How could he save the nation if he *didn't* escape with the virus? He would retreat now to advance later. And besides, after he'd risen to power, he would be able to represent this incident in rather more glamorous colours. History, as everyone knew, was written by the victorious.

And he'd return to the Pendragon Project too, one day, and destroy it utterly, along with everyone in it. They'd pay for their impertinence in challenging the saviour of Britain.

Beyond the Seal, like a great steel cork in the neck of the bottle that was the complex, dimly-lit and disused tunnels wound through rock to the elevators that finally granted access to the surface. Knight ordered most of his remaining men to maintain a defensive line at the Seal itself, to hold the scientists back while he and the others pushed on. Boudica accompanied him, of course, along with Ben, Tower, Garvey, and two hand-picked lieutenants. And the virus.

As they ran through the tunnels Knight radioed ahead. His helicopter would be waiting. Nothing could intervene between him and it.

'What's that . . . rumbling?' Boudica said.

It sounded like a landslide. The capsules of virus trembled in Frankie Garvey's hands.

Ahead of them, the tunnel wall imploded. Something gleaming and metallic slithered out of the rock and came to rest. Knight had never seen a terraprobe before, but as its protective bubble slid back, he was certainly acquainted with its rider.

'Nelligan!'

'Hi. Didn't want you to think I'd forgotten you, Bart.' He fired his shock blaster. The two hand-picked lieutenants were knocked off their feet.

'Tower! Ben!' glared Knight. 'Finish him!' The bodyguards raised their weapons. 'Not with guns, you'll risk the virus. *Tear* him to pieces!'

With instant obedience, the two giants pounded

towards Eddie. The ground shook beneath them. In the sickly yellow light and leaping shadows they seemed taller, huger than ever, crammed between floor and ceiling. Their arms swung down on him like falling tree trunks.

Eddie wasn't going to waste time. He knew why Knight didn't want gunfire, but there was no way he could miss either of *these* targets. He just didn't want to be underneath them when Tower and Ben were stunned into submission.

The shock blasts struck them perfectly in the middle of their prodigiously muscled chests.

They didn't even flinch.

And Eddie didn't get a second chance.

He hauled himself sidewards to elude the mighty swipe of Tower's battering-ram fist. They were simply too *big* now for a stun blast to affect, too strong. He needed to rethink strategy – as Ben's fists hammered the rock all too close to Eddie's head, shattering it like two pneumatic drills – and quickly.

He rolled over, kind of limped rather than leaped to his feet, feeling fire shoot through his injured leg. Typical Nelligan luck. Now was not the ideal time to have one's movement impaired, however slightly. Tower was on him, his flailing arms like the sails of a psychotic wind-mill. Eddie darted and ducked between the blows. Tried to launch some of his own.

But the giants were virtually invulnerable. And though it wasn't too hard to keep out of their lumbering way, they were forcing him back towards the project – he could hear the sounds of combat echoing from further down the tunnel – while Knight, Boudica and Garvey made good their escape.

Eddie couldn't let that happen. The giants had to have a weakness, an Achilles heel . . .

They were mountainous now, too heavy, larger and weightier than a man had a right to be. Eddie placed his faith in his shock blaster once again.

'You'd better give up, squirt,' jeered Ben, 'and we promise we'll keep it nice and painless. Yank your head clean off. Won't feel a thing.'

'Or what?' Eddie retorted. 'You'll grind my bones to make your bread? But talking of not feeling a thing . . .' He squeezed the trigger, hard, didn't let go. A barrage of shock blasts crackled at the giants' ankles. '. . . I'm afraid you *will*.'

The blaster froze the tendons, already under significant strain from Goliath body-weights. Ben lurched. Tower tottered. Their ankles gave way.

Bartholomew Knight's bodyguards crashed to earth.

'You just take a rest, boys,' Eddie grinned, 'though I don't reckon you'd be able to get up again even if you wanted to. Not without a crane. Now if you'll excuse me . . .'

He had a psychopath to catch.

And he chased through the tunnel ignoring the fact that his leg seemed to be working in a furnace. He couldn't be too late. He had to reach the elevators before Knight . . .

They were up ahead. Four of them. Knight, Boudica and Garvey were already in one, the doors still open like they were waiting for someone. Maybe Tower and Ben. Not Eddie.

'Knight, you piece of slime!' Eddie fired his blaster. He didn't seem to care that he might hit the virus capsule. 'You're not going anywhere!'

And then Garvey was throwing something at him. For one paralysing second Eddie thought it was a virus capsule. But no, he was all right.

It was only a grenade.

He launched himself for cover but the explosion still rammed into him like a solid force, like Tower's fist. Now the rest of him was burning in sympathy with his leg. His senses were scattered. He had to pull them back together. Had to stop squirming on the floor. Had to get up. Had to stop Knight and Boudica and . . .

Through a scarlet haze, as if his vision had been turned to blood, he saw the elevator doors closing. Knight was waving. They were laughing at him.

He'd failed again.

'No.' Eddie struggled to his knees, trying to stand, trying to do what he should. But the red was turning black and he'd lost his body somewhere and he'd lost Bartholomew Knight, too.

When he recovered consciousness Professor Syme and some of the other scientists were with him. There was more bad news.

They'd overpowered Knight's men. Righteous fury proving more than a match for mercenary self-interest – the masses of weapons stockpiled in the project hadn't done any harm, either. Knight's minions had either fallen or surrendered. But there'd been casualties too among the Pendragon scientists.

One of them was Professsor Henry Warwick.

Eddie was taken to him in the sick bay. He could see that it was bad, the bandages around the man's emaci-ated chest not disguising the gravity of the hole in his chest. His face was ashen. The light leaking from his eyes. Eddie had seen it before and it occurred to him sombrely that all the while he remained in the Deveraux organisation he would certainly see it again. There was no hope. Rose's father was a dead man.

Maybe she knew it too. She was sitting by his bedside cradling his head like a premature baby and she was valiantly trying not to cry. Warwick himself seemed certainly aware of the truth. He beckoned for Eddie to approach him as if he had something urgent to impart.

'I need to talk to Eddie, Rose,' he said. 'Privately. For a moment.'

Rose nodded and, with a tearful appeal to Eddie, withdrew.

'Knight escaped,' the professor observed without criticism.

Eddie took Rose's place. 'Not for long, sir. We'll get him. *I'll* get him.'

'But I won't be here to see it.' A resigned smile toyed with Warwick's grey lips. 'It seems I won't live to feel the sun on my skin after all.'

'Don't talk like that, Professor. You're going to be fine . . .'

'We both know that is not the case, Eddie, and we have no time to pretend otherwise. I'm dying. And perhaps it's better this way. My life has been a futile and a hollow one, the cause for which I was born has proved false, fruitless. The Pendragon Project – I see it clearly now – is an abomination. It is right that I should perish with it.'

'Professor Warwick, please . . .'

'But there has been one good thing in my life at least,

Eddie. One wonderful thing. Rose. You must promise me that you'll take care of her after I'm gone. Take her to the surface, let her live in sunlight for the rest of her days. I know you have feelings for her, Eddie. Act on them. Promise me you will. Rose is so very precious.'

'I promise,' Eddie said, with a conviction he'd only felt a handful of times in his life so far. 'I'll look after her, Professor Warwick. I will.'

'That's good, because there's one last thing I need to tell you, before the words no longer matter.' Their volume was fading now. Eddie had to lean closer to hear each syllable. 'I told you – when I still did not entirely trust you – that there was no anti-body for the Pendragon Virus.' Eddie's heart quickened. 'I did not tell you the truth.'

'You mean there *is* a cure?'

'Rose . . . is our only hope . . . the prettiest rose in all England . . .'

He was slipping away. Not *yet*, Eddie prayed. Hold on. 'The virus, Professor. The anti-body. What is it?'

'Our only hope,' Henry Warwick repeated faintly. 'The secret . . .'

Eddie pressed his ear almost to the Professor's mouth to detect his next words. It was as well he did. He could hardly believe them even then.

But the dying man was smiling. 'Rose now! . . . I want my Rose . . .'

'I'm here, Father.' Rose resumed her vigil. 'You just lie here and rest now. That's it. You just lie here and sleep.'

Eddie backed away tactfully. His belt and its communicator had been found, and he stepped outside the sick bay to contact Bowler. He was grateful he wasn't having to report Bartholomew Knight's escape face-to-face, but Bowler took the news without the slightest hint of recrimination. 'We were aware of sudden activity at the complex's entrance and the arrival of a helicopter,' he said. 'But before we could intercept the machine Mr Knight must have activated a stealth device. We lost it. Therefore, Master Edward, any culpability for the man's continued freedom from custody must, I am afraid, be shared.'

'You're not just trying to make me feel better, are you?' Eddie suspected.

'Master Edward,' observed Bowler, 'pandering to the failings of agents in the field would hardly be professional. Now, is it appropriate for us to join you underground?'

'Sure,' said Eddie. 'The techs are gonna love it but me, I can't wait to get out.' A sudden wail of grief broke from the sick bay. Eddie felt his own heart wring. 'Listen, Bowler, I've got to go. There's something . . . I'll tell you later . . .'

He had to comfort Rose. He was all she had now, her only friend in a world she didn't know.

He entered the sick bay, saw her lying across the lifeless body of her father, her slim form racked with sobs. Poor Professor Warwick. His death marked the end of the Pendragon Project but not, Eddie vowed, the end of his mission. It was just one more reason why Knight was going to pay.

TWELVE

IGC DATA-FILE 2066
SUB-SECTION: GREAT BRITAIN MEDIA FEED

The location of UK First Party leader
Bartholomew Knight and his daughter Boudica
remains a mystery. Police refuse to confirm that
they are being sought in conjunction with
offences under the Prevention of Terrorism Act,
though anybody who has any information as to
their possible whereabouts is asked to contact
the authorities.

Meanwhile, security continues to increase in
advance of the Treaty of Europa Conference in
three days' time. Albion has declared that even
if the conference begins, it will never be
allowed to finish. Prime Minister Peregrine
Barnes has dismissed the organisation's threats
in robust terms, however. 'These people represent nobody but themselves and their own twisted
agendas. Albion is trying to resist the tide of

history which, like King Canute attempting to
hold back the sea, cannot be done. Our nation
stands on the threshold of a glorious moment. We
must not turn back now.'

London's hospitals are poised to accept
unprecedented numbers of casualties in the
event of a terrorist atrocity during the period
of the conference. Extra staff are already
standing by.

The doctors were not pleased when Rose was nowhere
to be found, and Eddie could understand why. But they
could still have cut her some slack. She'd buried her
father only yesterday. 'Don't panic,' he calmed them.
'She can't have gone far. I'll fetch her.'

She was wandering in the hospital grounds. Eddie saw
her examining bushes and flowers as if they were examples of exotic alien flora which, he supposed, to her they
pretty much were. The Pendragon Project hadn't been
good for growth, human or botanical. 'Rose,' he said,
crossing to her.

She offered him the wistful, slightly apologetic smile
that had become customary with her since the death of
her father, a smile that contained within itself the impli-
cation that it had no right to exist in a tragic world. A
smile that made him want to hold her and whisper that
things would get better.

'It's time, Rose. The docs are asking for you.'

Rose nodded. 'Sorry, Eddie. I just came out here to
think. Impressive, isn't it, that I should come *outside* to
think? I'm not afraid of the surface world now, not the
way I was.'

'That's good, Rose. I knew it'd only be time.'

'Did you know the survivors of the project are all going to be housed together for the moment, until we're ready to make a new life for ourselves? We're going to be taught all about the world of 2066. We're going to be shown how to fit in and be normal.'

'I had heard that, yeah.'

'Only one thing still worries me,' Rose admitted, casting Eddie a cautious glance. 'What does fitting in and being normal mean here on the surface? In the project we were few, our world was small, and we all had clearly defined roles and a purpose. Here, there are so many people, countless people, and everything is so vast and unpredictable. I don't feel like I matter anymore, Eddie. I feel lost. I feel alone.'

'You're not alone, Rose,' Eddie reassured her, touching her arm to prove it. 'You've got me.'

'Have I?' Hopefulness and doubt contending. 'I suppose fitting in and being normal includes boyfriends, does it?'

'I guess it could do,' said Eddie. 'If you're a girl. Are you advertising the position?'

'I don't know what you mean.'

'Because I'd like to apply. My references may not be great but . . .'

'Eddie, please.' Rose's brow furrowed. 'Don't make fun of me.'

'I'd never make fun of you, Rose.' His own brow following suit. 'I'm just trying to tell you, with typical Nelligan lameness, that you're not alone. I want to be with you. I want you to be my girl.'

'But, Eddie, how *can* you?'

'How can I? From where I'm standing it's pretty easy . . .'

'But I mean Boudica. I saw there was something between you before.' Rose was pained, insecure. 'And she's so beautiful. How can you prefer someone like me to her?'

'How?' Eddie laughed, squeezed Rose tight. 'Even if I didn't happen to think you make Boudica Knight look like the model for a Halloween fright mask, which I do, it's not just about looks. It's about what's inside: personality, feelings, who you are. Boudica's a psycho. *You're* the one for me, Rose, the only one.' They were clenched together. 'So don't expect me to let go any time soon.'

'But I don't know what to do, Eddie, I don't know what to say. The only boy of my age in the project was only interested in explosives. I've never been with anyone.' An embarrassed blush. 'I've never even kissed a boy. Not properly. Not the way . . . you know . . .'

'Well, that is outrageous,' Eddie grinned. 'We'll have to put that right immediately.'

'You want to kiss me?'

'Is the world round?'

'I want to kiss you, too.' She stretched up to him.

And the likes of Boudica, Bella, even Bex, Eddie could consign them to the past without regret. His future, as Bex had predicted, belonged to Rose.

'I only wish my Dad was here,' she said a few moments later, as if ashamed that even for a second she'd forgotten her sadness.

Eddie recollected himself as well, and why he'd come looking for her. 'Well, there's still something you need to do for him,' he said, 'and it's going to ensure he'll be remembered for saving lives, for helping us to catch Knight. The doctors?'

'I'm ready,' said Rose. 'But will you come with me, Eddie?'

'Just you try and stop me.'

IGC DATA-FILE 2066
SUB-SECTION: GREAT BRITAIN MEDIA FEED

The construction of the Millennium Halls transformed what had been an industrial wasteland since the turn of the century into the site of a complex of striking grace and beauty. Much of it was composed of glasteel, the revolutionary material that combines the translucency of glass with the strength of steel. The shimmering glasteel walls of the Millennium Halls were designed to admit as much natural light as possible, thus symbolising the purpose of the structure: to further and advance the light of understanding between peoples and nations. This noble intention achieves its most dramatic expression with the Main Debating Chamber and the attached Communication Spire. The latter, open to the public when debates are not taking place, soars eight hundred metres into the air and is built entirely from glasteel - a gleaming needle pointing to the skies that seems to embody the highest aspirations of humankind. At the summit, gained by the most spectacular elevator ride in the world, there is a circular viewing gallery open to the air and a transmitter broadcasting messages of peace to the world in a hundred languages twenty-four hours a day. The key meetings of the Treaty of Europa Conference, however, will be held in the crystal cathedral of the Main Debating Chamber itself. It is in this magnificent room that the future direction of the United Kingdom will be determined. On this, the first morning of the Conference, more than 4,000 police officers are deployed in a so-called ring of steel around the Millennium Halls in order to prevent protestors from getting too close. Many of the Europan delegates are arriving by helicopter, and security at the complex's helipad is also tight.

Prime Minister Peregrine Barnes was in optimistic mood when he spoke to journalists before leaving for the halls. 'This is a most auspicious day, not solely for the United Kingdom but for Europa as well. It will soon be apparent how much we already have in common and how little we would lose by making our cultural, historical and social ties political in nature, too. And yes, I know this conference has been threatened, but to the terrorists of Albion I say this, once and for all: we do not fear you. We do not heed you. And nothing you do will deter us from making the *right* decision for Britain.'

'Not just fingerprints, Rose,' said Eddie, 'but retinal scans, too. Nobody's going to get in here who isn't who they say they are – not unless they've got an artificial head or something.'

'So there's nothing to worry about, then?' Rose said hopefully.

'Shouldn't be.' Eddie and Rose stood in the central concourse of the Millennium Halls watching a melee of delegate politicians, journalists and anyone else whose business it was to be here passing through the security checkpoints. Armed police were also prominent. 'On the other hand, they did say the *Titanic* was unsinkable, and we all know what happened there. All the while Knight's still at large, I don't think we can take chances.'

'Even if we know something he doesn't know,' smiled Rose.

'Even if.'

'Well *I'm* not worried. Not with you here to look after us, Eddie.' She slipped her hand into his and kissed him lightly on the cheek.

'Please, not while I'm on duty.' He wore his sleepshot wristbands and there was a shock blaster in his shoulder holster, but no shocksuit. It had been deemed inappropriate for Eddie to stand out so obviously. Quiet, unobtrusive undercover work was the order of the day unless and until Knight put in an appearance. It was a bonus that Rose had been granted security clearance to join him, just in case something went wrong with Plan A and she was needed.

'Excuse me. Sir?' The pair were approached by a group of five men and one woman, carrying laptops and briefcases. Their name-tags identified them as members of the delegation from the Europan Region of Luxemburg. 'One moment, please. You are official?'

'Official? Yeah, I guess we are, wouldn't you say, Miss Warwick?'

The man who'd spoken, a man with a beard like a hibernating bear-cub, nodded vigorously as though intent on proving his friendship. 'What a marvellous thing it is to be here, is it not, sir? A marvellous occasion. My fellow delegates and I have been looking most forward to this day for a very long time. History will be made this day, sir, do you not agree?'

'Most probably,' Eddie said. 'Can we help you?'

'Ah, yes.' The man waggled a finger. 'The main debating chamber. Would you be happening to know where we can find it?'

'You could just follow the crowd,' Eddie pointed out, but in the spirit of international cooperation that the conference was supposed to be fostering, he went on to give directions.

'Thank you so much, sir. Thank you so much.' The man with the beard pumped his hand like Eddie had just saved his life. His fellow delegates followed his lead. 'It has been a pleasure to meet you and this charming young lady. Your sister? No? Well, perhaps we will see you later, yes?'

'I vote for no,' muttered Eddie as the delegation departed. He checked his watch. 'This is where we split up, Rose. I've got to join Bowler in the body of the chamber and keep my eyes open. You get to sit in the public gallery and drop off to sleep if you like. See you later.' He kissed her rather more quickly have he'd have liked.

'I thought you said not while you're on duty,' Rose complained playfully.

'A good secret agent knows when to break the rules.' Eddie crossed his hands and pointed both left and right. 'Thisaway. Thataway. Bye.'

Rose watched her boyfriend leave. Her *boyfriend*. An almost impossible concept until recently. Yet here she was, on the surface, never likely to return to the Pendragon Project again. Her life had altered intrinsically and irreversibly. What lay ahead of her now she could not imagine, but she knew that an essential part of it would be Eddie. She followed him with her eyes until he turned a corner and disappeared from view. With a sigh, she supposed that she should set off herself.

Only she was distracted. It was indeed time for the conference to commence, and just about everybody entitled to had moved to the main debating chamber, leaving the surrounding crystal corridors almost deserted. *Just* about everybody. And *almost* deserted.

The Luxemburg delegation were heading in the opposite direction, and seemed intent on continuing to do so. She smiled. It made her feel good that she should find her way about on the surface more readily than some of those who'd been born here. She was fitting in and being normal.

She'd help the hapless delegates out.

'Excuse me. Excuse me.' She chased after them and with the recent migration of the other delegates her voice almost echoed beneath the glass ceiling. 'You're going the wrong way.' Towards the lower levels, it seemed.

Why would they want to go there?

'Ah, it's *you* again,' said the bearded man, somehow less friendly than before. 'How fortuitous. And we're going the wrong way, are we?'

'Yes. I thought . . . as I saw you . . .' They were suddenly closing around her. Their smiles somehow false, somehow plastic. 'The debating chamber is . . .' She indicated feebly.

'Ah, but you see, there is your mistake, Rose.' How did he know her name? It only said Miss R Warwick on her badge. 'We're not going to the debating chamber.' *Eddie, where are you?* 'We have business in the Oxygen Control Centre first, thanks to your father's virus.'

'Knight,' breathed Rose.

Hands seized her from behind, clapped across her mouth, prevented her from screaming. She clutched for Bartholomew Knight, sank her fingernails into his cheek and tore. He chuckled. The skin peeled away but there was no blood.

'Let me help you, my dear,' he said graciously. 'It was highly amusing to deceive yourself and the wretched Nelligan earlier, but this face has now outworn its usefulness.' He worked his fingers into his eye-sockets and twisted and pulled and ripped. His eyes fell out, shattered on the floor. Lenses patterned to someone else's retina. The mask came away in shreds, the beard in ludicrous tufts. Bartholomew Knight peeked out from beneath.

Rose's eyes widened as the rest of the delegation stripped off their false identities. Frankie Garvey. Boudica. The hired muscle. She was in real trouble now.

'Let's just kill her, Father,' Boudica recommended bitterly.

'Not yet,' cautioned Garvey. 'She might still have her uses. What do you think, Mr Knight? We can always finish her later.'

'Bring her,' Knight ruled. 'She at least deserves to see her father's creation in all its glory. Now come. Our moment of destiny awaits.'

Rose was virtually carried by arms too strong for her to resist as Knight's group strode swiftly to the Oxygen Control Centre. If she could only shout, yell, warn someone somehow. The hand over her mouth, it was damp and sweaty, making her gorge rise. But it gave her the only plan she could think of. Holding back her revulsion, Rose bit down on the calloused flesh. *Hard*.

The man cried out involuntarily. His grip weakened momentarily. It was enough. Rose wrested herself frantically from his grasp, hit the ground running. 'He's here! Knight's here!' She charged manically along the corridor, took a left. The OCC was ahead. 'He's here!' Guards outside, startled at the sudden appearance of a screaming girl, lifted their weapons. Too slowly.

Shock blasts sent them spinning back against the wall.

Rose stared in silent horror at the dead guards. Knight was behind her, the nozzle of his gun cold against the back of her neck. It was all over. Did you hear the shot that killed you, she wondered? Her mouth opened to utter its final sound.

Knight brought his shock blaster down on her skull. Rose felt her head explode, her vision fragment like broken glass, and she felt herself crumpling, collapsing, no strength in her legs. But she also felt herself *alive*.

Admittedly, in a nightmare. The violence blurred around her as she tried to rouse herself from the floor. The doors to the OCC blasted open. Knight, his men and Boudica rushed in. Shock blasts and screams rumbled against her hearing like distant thunder. She glimpsed techs, their white coats stained red. Saw guards, writhing in space, falling through air. Then someone dragging her inside.

Knight was barking orders. 'Seal all the airlocks,

every last entrance and exit. There are to be no survivors.'

And then he was beside her, holding a black egg in his hand. 'The Pendragon Virus,' he crooned, like the name of a lover. 'Thank your father for this the next time you see him, won't you, Rose?'

'My father is dead.' Her voice reduced to a croak.

'Is he?' Knight seemed unmoved. 'Well, thanks to this little capsule here, many more will soon be joining him. We're going to use the oxygen generators to add a certain something extra to the atmosphere. Guess what?'

'You wouldn't . . .'

'I would. I will,' promised Knight. 'To save the country I love, to preserve my way of life, I will do *anything.*'

'Do it now, Father,' urged Boudica.

Knight drew himself up to his full, commanding height. 'Put on your filters. Put one on her, too.'

The briefcases that Knight's group had carried when posing as the Luxemburg delegation contained not documents or papers but bulkier versions of the Deveraux belt-breathers with which Rose was already familiar. These covered the nose and mouth and were strapped around the back of the head.

Knight prepared to break the capsule.

'From here,' he said, inhuman through the mask's microphone, 'the virus will be spread throughout the Millennium Halls in less than a minute. In the same time again, the Prime Minister who would betray this nation, his acolytes, the corrupt representatives of foreign power and all their obsequious underlings in the media and the security services, all will perish. In two minutes, the era of Bartholomew Knight will begin.'

'No!' cried Rose.

'Yes!' countered Knight.

Exerting pressure on the virus capsule. Closing his fist inexorably.

'. . . No . . .' Rose couldn't look. She didn't dare. But it happened anyway.

And the alarms shrilled as the pure air of the Millennium Halls was contaminated, and if anyone but Bartholomew Knight had been in occupation of the Oxygen Control Centre, then the safety protocols and the section isolation systems might still have preserved some areas of the complex from the ravages of the contagion. But they could not.

Rose watched Knight celebrating what he'd done and wondered how they could be members of the same species.

The Pendragon Virus was loose.

THIRTEEN

They began to see the bodies as they approached the main debating chamber – slumped against the wall, spreadeagled on the floor or curled up in balls like overgrown foetuses. The bodies were of people who'd worked at the Millennium Halls first, and who now looked as if they wished their career path had extended in a different direction. Then security guards, still holding their guns with limp fingers. A reporter who, sadly for him, had become part of the story. A trail of atrocity to pick their way along.

'Incredible,' admired Bartholomew Knight. 'We will go down in history after this. My name will be remembered for ever.'

'Just like Hitler's,' Rose predicted.

'Shut up!' snapped Boudica, prodding Rose with her shock blaster. 'I'm happy for you, Father. And you,' returning her vitriolic attention to Rose, 'I want you to be thinking about Eddie first, and how he's lying somewhere not very far from here, the virus eating away at his lungs, and how he's never going to make a wisecrack again. And then I want you to be thinking about me second, and what I'm going to do to you once we get out of here.'

'Fear not, Boudica,' said her father confidently. 'Our transportation is already on its way. Let the lamentable authorities break through the entrances we sealed if they dare. They will not avoid the virus. By the time they realise the necessity for masks, we will be long gone. With one final bonus.' The small group reached one of the several sets of double doors, all at present closed, that led directly into the main debating chamber. 'The chance to see our enemies laid low.'

Bartholomew Knight pushed open the doors and they entered. The chamber was indeed as impressive as the Millennium Halls' literature claimed. More of an arch than a dome, it was constructed almost entirely of glasteel. On its far side an elevator provided access to the Communication Spire which could be seen through the sloping roof spearing for the skies like the wake of a spaceship. A public gallery formed a semi-circle many rows high facing a vast round table inlaid with computers where the dignitaries sat and discussed the great issues of the day. There was little debate going on right now among the men and women at the table, however, not that those who had come to listen seemed to care. Death tends to readjust priorities.

'Wow.' Frankie Garvey sounded like a child visiting the Magic Kingdom for the first time. 'I've never seen anything like this before. What old Alazi would have done for a capsule of the Pendragon Virus!'

Bartholomew Knight marched to the centre of the chamber with the formality of a man in church. 'They brought this upon themselves,' he declared. 'By turning their backs on two thousand years of history. By turning away from all that made Britain great: our culture, our heritage. By seeking to make us something we are not.' His voice rose as if in hope that the sleepers would hear him. 'But I am Bartholomew Knight. The nation speaks through me. This land has chosen me to be its saviour and its lord. And today is just the beginning.'

'You mean you're not gonna shut up yet?'

The mood in Knight's party changed abruptly. Shock blasters jabbed to readiness. Boudica grabbed Rose's arm as she joined the others in a defensive circle.

But that didn't stop the red-haired girl from laughing out his name: 'Eddie!'

'Nelligan?' Knight was baffled. 'Impossible.'

'Very possible, I'm afraid.' They saw him, sitting up from where he'd apparently been lying dead. 'The word resurrection mean anything to you?'

And he wasn't alone. The whole chamber was stirring. There was movement at the debating table and waking in the public gallery.

'No?' Eddie pursued. 'What about the word anti-body, as in anti-body for the Pendragon Virus?'

They were surrounded. Knight saw security guards rush Peregrine Barnes out of harm's immediate way. They were outnumbered.

'But . . . there *is* no anti-body. Warwick said so.'

'Change of plan. There *is* one. It's in Rose's blood. *Rose* is the cure for the virus, and everyone who has a right to be here has already been inoculated. As soon as we heard the alarms, we played dead and waited for you to come to us. And hey, here you are. Now put your blasters down and let Rose go.' How Knight had managed to capture her Eddie couldn't afford to care. It was ensuring her safety that mattered now. 'Do you hear me, Knight? It's all over.'

'Of course it is.' Bartholomew Knight smiled insidiously. 'I seem to have been outwitted.' He began to raise his hands.

'Not up. Down!' ordered Eddie. 'Drop the blasters *now*!'

'When I tell you,' hissed Knight to his companions.

'Eddie!' Rose cried. 'They're going to . . .'

Fire.

There was chaos in the debating chamber. Delegates and reporters and officials alike squawked for the exits. They'd done their bit for the day in the war against global terror. Eddie, an equally revived Bowler and the rest of the security personnel, however, still had work to do. Beginning with taking out Bartholomew Knight.

Their initial volley eliminated one of his minions, the impact driving the man backwards over the debating table, but the others fought with a frenzy born of desperation. And unlike Eddie and his allies, they didn't care who they shot. Several fleeing delegates went down; more were used for cover. Rose was flourished like a shield in front of Boudica and her father, Frankie Garvey loyally guarding their backs.

'Don't fire if you risk hitting Rose!' Eddie yelled, battling his way past the retreating delegates, looking for a clear opening. He wasn't getting one.

Knight was moving with purpose, his group focussing their energies now on carving a path that led to the Communication Spire.

Eddie knew why. It was why Jonathan Deveraux had granted him the authority to set the trap the way he had. It was always possible Knight could sneak into the Halls somehow, disguised or something as he'd evidently done, but if he got as far as liberating the virus, he certainly wouldn't be able to sneak out again. He'd have to have an alternative means of exit, a way out that wasn't guarded by half the police in England. Like the viewing gallery at the top of the Spire.

Eddie remembered Boudica showing him around the Knights' private jet and the compartment he'd joked was like a futuristic shower. 'Tractor beam,' he cursed to himself. 'They'll use the tractor beam.' And they still had Rose.

They couldn't get away again. He couldn't fail *again*. A defining moment was upon him, Eddie felt it like a solid weight on his shoulders, one of those moments that he and his fellow Spy High students had been warned would come, sooner or later and perhaps many times during their careers, critical moments that would test not only their physical skills but their will, their purpose, the strength of their resolve. Prove yourself moments, Senior Tutor Grant had called them.

Eddie needed to prove himself.

He went down on one knee. Pumped blast after blast at Knight's lackeys. One fell. But they'd reached the elevator doors. Knight was opening them. Eddie had a final chance to save Rose as the surviving minion held her while Boudica darted into the elevator car. A final shot. He aimed, made his mark huge in his mind, relegated the surrounding chaos to silence and absence. The next time Rose pulled to her right . . .

He squeezed the trigger. The shock blast sent the underling staggering backwards. Rose threw herself to the floor. He could maybe hit Knight himself now.

But his shot ricocheted from the glasteel elevator doors as they closed.

Eddie was by Rose's side in seconds. 'I'm all right. I'm all right.' She shrugged off his concern. 'Do what you need to do, Eddie. Get Knight.'

'I will,' Eddie vowed, 'then it'll just be you and me. Bowler – ' turning to his liaison man who was magically alongside him – 'status report on the doors. Why aren't they open?'

'It appears Mr Knight has scrambled the control systems, Master Edward,' Bowler confessed. 'I'm afraid it will take a few minutes to *un*scramble them.'

'We don't have a few minutes.' Eddie frowned up at the elevator car, clearly visible as it scaled the spire, as if providing a trio of tourists with happy holiday memories. 'As soon as Knight's plane is hovering in position, they'll be tractor-beaming out of here. We'll have to smash through the wall and I'll take the stairs.' He flipped his shock blaster to Materials. 'Don't worry, Bowler. I got an A in the Sitting Duck Pursuit Module back at Spy High.'

'That's very impressive, Master Edward,' acknowledged Bowler, 'but even so, might one suggest an alternative?'

Bartholomew Knight had clearly taken into account the significant likelihood that he would not be simply allowed to depart unchallenged. As Eddie and an uncannily fit Bowler raced out to the heli-pad, it was raining swarm-shells. All around there was carnage, the concrete surface pitted and fissured, many of the choppers themselves already aflame or incapable of flight, men running, panicking, crying out – a scene of devastation shrouded in clouds of black smoke.

'Just as well we don't need a helicopter,' remarked Eddie. 'Time for me to rise above the situation.'

He clamped the jet pack in place over his shoulders. It was regulation Spy High issue. The directional units jutted out on either side of his head, the magnetic thrusters tapered down his back, the control arms awaited his instructions at his waist. He glanced up at the spire, its shimmering peak impervious to the commotion below, the elevator at the viewing gallery. Knight within sight of safety.

'Get their plane intercepted, Bowler,' Eddie urged, booting up the jet pack, 'though I've got one or two ideas about that myself.' He patted his belt. 'Wish me luck.'

'A competent secret agent, Master Edward,' observed Bowler, 'is not dependent on fortune to complete his mission.' Eddie's response was lost as he rose into the air and towards the spire. He didn't hear Bowler's final comment, either, uncharacteristically fervent. 'But good luck anyway, Master Edward. Good luck indeed.'

They emerged on to the viewing gallery and, now that they were in uncontaminated air, immediately dispensed with their masks. Frankie Garvey's eyes glinted as he saw the destruction wrought by the swarm-shells. Boudica chose to scan the skies instead. 'Father, shouldn't the plane be here by now? Father?'

'Perhaps it would be better if it didn't arrive at all,' spat Bartholomew Knight.

'What?' Both his younger companions now fixed their attention solely on him, but only his daughter spoke. 'Father, what do you mean?'

'You need to ask?' He spared her the briefest of contemptuous glances. 'After the humiliation of our failure, our ignominious retreat?'

'But Father,' Boudica encouraged, 'once we've escaped we can make new plans. We can strike again. We still have the Pendragon Virus.'

'And they, daughter, have the anti-virus.' Knight's expression grew darker, more brooding. 'No, *this* was to have been our defining moment, the moment we proved ourselves. Our time was today, the conference. England expects every man to do his duty but I was unable to do mine. I thought to join the pantheon of British heroes, to add my name to the list of the noble few who gave their all to make this country great, but I have brought only disgrace to our cause. My name means nothing.'

'No, Father.' Boudica seized his hand, the one that wasn't holding the shock blaster. 'That's not true. You're *still* a great man. You can still do great *things*, make your mark on history. With me by your side.'

'But you're my daughter, Boudica . . .' Knight seemed unpersuaded.

'Frankie agrees with me, don't you, Frankie?' Boudica appealed.

'Oh, sure, sure.' Though perhaps Garvey was reconsidering. Not his basic philosophy that the world's population was neatly divided into weak and strong, but exactly who was weak and who was strong, particularly in relation to his present employer. There was little time for further reflection, however. 'Look!'

'Is it the tractor beam?' But Boudica could see nothing, and in any case Garvey was pointing downwards. She followed the direction of his finger. 'No,' she groaned.

It wasn't the tractor beam. It was Eddie.

Jet-packing towards an enemy, you always had a choice. You could go for maximum manoeuvrability, especially useful when under fire, by keeping both hands on the control arms and exploiting every inch of flexibility your directional units could offer. Or you could opt for the 'attack is the best form of defence' approach, and sacrifice a little movement in favour of allocating one hand to a shock blaster.

Tens of metres above the ground now, zeroing in on Knight, Boudica and Garvey, Eddie favoured the latter. Not, he sought to assure himself, because doing so gave him the chance to eliminate his old rival with a stun blast, but because the Communication Spire itself could be used for additional cover. The viewing gallery was broader than the central tower, jutted out over it. Eddie would be seen beneath the terrorists' feet, but the strength of the glasteel floor ensured he would not be *shot*.

Providing he got that far.

Garvey's fire sizzled the air around him, but wasn't too difficult to avoid. Eddie was like a skier on a sky-borne slalom course. 'I love you too, Frankie!' he yelled, retaliating with blasts that flashed and flared against the rim of the viewing gallery. A tad higher, and they'd be flashing and flaring against Garvey's head.

But now the Knights were joining in, creating a crossfire that was altogether more demanding to elude. With blasts from three directions instead of one, Eddie's concentration had to be absolute. He had to ignore the crazy hatred on Knight's face, the indignant rage on Boudica's. He had to remember – all three dimensions were at his mercy. Most people were unused to seeing their targets moving up and down as well as sideways. It took them a little while to adapt. Little whiles saved agents' lives. As the Knights and Garvey redirected their aim, Eddie winged his way to the shelter of the central tower.

He could see them, cursing him through transparent glasteel like he was hiding in an ocean. He thought he'd better rise to the surface. Glimmering far above, from a plane that could not be seen, a tractor beam was descending.

Eddie boosted his acceleration, angled himself diagonally out from the column of the spire, shock blaster at the ready.

'Give it up, Knight!' he shouted. 'There's no way out for you!'

The three on the viewing gallery seemed to think otherwise. Not perhaps surprisingly, given the sudden appearance of the tractor beam, like a staircase from heaven, enticingly only metres from them. But *behind* them, while Eddie, now with the advantage of height, was shooting down.

Knight backed away, still firing. Eddie didn't aim at him but at the floor beyond. Knight stumbled into the cascade of shock blasts. His legs temporarily crumbled beneath him. He fell.

'Father!' Boudica was at his side instantly.

Not good for Garvey. So Boudica Knight would sooner tend to her old man like a soft-hearted nurse than continue the fight against their enemy. Weak or strong? Which was that? Maybe he'd overestimated the Knights. Maybe he'd *under*estimated Eddie, who was coming dangerously close with those shock blasts.

Should he stay to help the wounded? That would definitely be weak.

But running for the tractor beam? That sounded strong to Frankie.

He unleashed a final burst of shock blasts at Eddie's right side, forcing him to swivel and momentarily cease firing. It allowed Garvey one of those little whiles that could serve a terrorist's cause just as helpfully as a secret agent's.

He turned and hurtled for the tractor beam, plunged into the blue sanctuary of its energy, felt himself lifted from the spire at once.

'Oh, no, you don't, Frankie,' muttered Eddie, swooping low over the viewing gallery. 'You're not getting away this time.' As he thrust his blaster under his belt and reached for something else, he recalled the grenade Garvey had hurled at him in the tunnels of the Pendragon Project. 'What goes around comes around. Here's to a nice long stay in a penal satellite.'

He lobbed the stun grenade into the tractor beam. The tractor beam did not distinguish between organic and inorganic objects. Up it went.

❋

Frankie Garvey emerged from blue light into the tractor beam compartment of Knight's plane. The beam's operator seemed to have been expecting someone else. 'Where's Mr Knight? And Boudica?'

'Don't worry about them,' Garvey snapped. They're weak, he thought. Leave them to Nelligan. 'Let's just get out of here. Tell the pilot.'

'But we can't go without Mr Knight,' the tractor beam operator appeared to believe.

'You'll do as I say. Now turn the beam off and let's move.'

'No.' The operator stood his ground. Might have wished he hadn't. In the five seconds it took Frankie Garvey to drag him aside, something else entered the compartment via the beam. Something explosive.

And Garvey's fingers, even as he registered the grenade's presence, were already depressing the controls.

The tractor beam was extinguished. The hatch closed.

The grenade dropped.

Eddie wasn't the only one atop the Communication Spire who knew what it meant when the tractor beam vanished and did not reappear.

'Afraid your flight's been cancelled,' he said, landing on the viewing gallery. 'And if you look below us, you'll see some nice, smartly uniformed security guards climbing up the stairs to take you into custody. You may as well put your blaster down, Boudica.' Not that Eddie did. 'It's all over.'

'Father?' Boudica's hand wavered.

'Yes, yes, do as he says.' Knight stayed on his knees. He seemed bowed, broken. He'd lost his own shock blaster and much else besides, it appeared. 'Nelligan is right. It *is* over, finished. Britain will be no more. Barnes will have his way now and soon our once-proud race will exist only as a subject people in a northern province of a state they neither understand nor love, helpless to govern their own lives or forge their own destiny. Oh, my country, your ardent son has failed you.'

'But, Father . . .' Boudica obediently placed her blaster on the floor. She was dismayed, afraid even. The father she had worshipped all her life had been mighty, invincible, an elemental force. Now, to see him reduced to this, seeming to shrink and age before her very eyes, it was too much to endure. 'Are you satisfied, Eddie?' she glared. 'Do you see what you've done? You've destroyed a great man here today.'

'Well, first off, I think yours and my definitions of greatness might be a little different, Boudica, and second off—' Eddie's tone hardened suddenly – 'could you put the keypad down, Mr Knight.' He'd produced the object from a jacket pocket surreptitiously and was pushing buttons with crafty quickness. 'I mean it. Put it down . . .'

Boudica stepped in front of her father. 'Or what, Eddie? You'll shoot me to get to Dad? Gun down an unarmed girl?'

His blaster was only set to stun, but psychologically, the idea of firing at Boudica in cold blood still caused hesitation. And then it was no longer necessary. Bartholomew Knight had tossed the keypad away. They saw it begin the eight hundred metre tumble to the ground. And Bartholomew Knight was laughing.

'What was that about, Knight?' Eddie sensed renewed danger. 'What did you just do?'

'What you required of me, Nelligan,' Knight claimed. 'I put down the keypad, the one that I used earlier to summon the swarm-shells. Of course, before I did so I also altered the trajectory of the remaining bombs.'

'What do you mean?' But Eddie had a good idea.

He felt the impact of swarm-shell on glasteel below, the spire shuddering as if in fear of its life. Instead of avoiding the tower, now the bombs were programmed to make it their primary target.

'I will not be taken,' Knight vowed. 'Bartholomew Knight will not be paraded through the streets, subjected to the mockery of a trial like a common criminal. No, he would sooner die than suffer such indignities.'

'Knight, don't be . . .'

The man was like lightning. He was seizing Boudica's gun, raising, firing it. Eddie felt a scorching pain in his right shoulder, like he'd been branded by a red-hot poker. He slumped against the side of the viewing gallery. Some kind of red liquid was running down his sleeve and he appeared to have misplaced his shock blaster. Through the sudden jolt of his agony, Eddie realised that Bartholomew Knight could kill him.

And amid a rush of explosions, each one a louder, nearer echo of the last, like a racing heartbeat, the Communication Spire, the mast of a sinking ship, began to list to the side.

'I could finish you now, Nelligan,' Knight declared, 'but I prefer to grant you the privilege of dying with us, of witnessing our moment of supreme sacrifice.'

'Dying?' Now it was Boudica's voice that wavered. 'With *us*?' There was something disturbing in her father's eyes, a kind of proud fatalism. She imagined that Joan of

Arc might have carried the same aspect with her to the stake. 'I don't understand.'

As glasteel walls split open with protesting shrieks. As the security men below no longer scaled the stairs, those who were still alive scrambling back the way they'd come.

'Of course you understand, Boudica, my precious child,' Knight said. 'You told me yourself, not minutes past, that I could still accomplish great things with you, my only daughter, by my side. What we do now will be remembered for ever.'

'But I don't want to die.' Boudica felt it fiercely, staring at a stranger in her father's form. 'I don't want to die, Father!'

'You won't die, my darling daughter.' Knight narrowed his eyelids serenely. 'Neither of us will die. We will live for ever in the memory of Britain.'

'Oh, my God,' Boudica wailed. 'Eddie!'

Eddie was struggling to recover, isolating the pain of his wound, ignoring it. So he was bleeding. He had pints left. So his right arm was numbed and useless. Nelson made do with one. He clambered to his feet again. And was that him swaying or the spire?

'Eddie, help me!' Boudica darted forward, tried to. Her father seized her arm, yanked her back and struck her across the face in a single fluently violent movement. Tears welled from her eyes to match the blood from her lip. 'You hit me.' In utter disbelief. 'You *hit* me.'

'I'm sorry. I didn't mean to. You *made* me,' Knight rationalised, 'by going to *him*. Perhaps he'd be less of a distraction dead after all . . .' He levelled his weapon.

Eddie wondered which would prove quicker, shock blaster or jet pack.

There was a rending roar as the tower tipped, lurched, subsided by metres. All three on the viewing gallery staggered, and Boudica was first to recover. She threw herself at her father's gun arm, wrestled with him for possession of the blaster. She couldn't do it alone. Eddie never thought he'd see the day when he and Boudica were fighting on the same side.

'Father, listen to me!'

'Knight, we can still make it if you . . .'

There was another glasteel groan. Another subsidence. And swarm-shells were no longer required. The spire had already sustained terminal damage. It reeled like the loser of a gun-fight about to collapse.

Knight's blaster was wrestled from his hand, clattered to the sloping floor, slid away from him. Mastering the pain in his shoulder, Eddie retrieved it.

'Now what say we stop playing games,' he winced, 'and let's see if I can jet pack you both to terra firma.'

Knight wasn't listening. He'd shaken Boudica off and was standing tall, indomitable, his eyes on the blaster and gloating. 'Do you want to kill me, Nelligan? You want to kill me, don't you? Well, here I am. I won't stop you. Because you can't kill me, Nelligan, do you realise that? I am immortal. I am part of the soul of this kingdom. I will live for ever in its dreams and in its memories like King Arthur himself, and one day, one day I will return.'

'Man, I hope not.' Eddie felt the platform vibrating beneath his feet. The jet pack was primed. The spire was about to give way. 'Last chance to live. Boudica?'

'Stay with me, Boudica,' Knight implored. 'Share your father's triumph.'

'Dad,' Boudica pleaded, 'I don't want to *die*!'

Like a cue.

The Communication Spire snapped in two, and suddenly the Knights were falling, plummeting, gravity dashing them to the ground like stones slung by a vindictive boy.

Only Eddie was immune. The jet pack stabilised him, held him up. He could save himself, but saving yourself was not what being a graduate of Spy High was about. He rocketed towards the exploding earth, exceeding the speed of gravity. He let the blaster go, had a better use for his one good hand, jabbed it out imploringly, fingers stretching. 'Boudica!'

She was screaming but she still reached out for him, she still had sense enough for that.

And their hands clasped. Their hands held. His arm was all but wrenched from its socket but he clung on and so did Boudica.

Her father was not so fortunate. They lost sight of him in the carnage as the spire avalanched in glasteel boulders on to the roof of the main debating chamber, crashing through and erupting again in pillars of fire and smoke. For Bartholomew Knight, there was no hope.

And now the strain was telling on Eddie's muscles. His wounded right arm alone could scarcely control their descent and besides, the jet pack was not designed for the weight of two. They were coming down too quickly. He was going to have to spiral, to slow their fall by funnelling it. 'Boudica!' he yelled. 'Try to . . . stay still . . .'

Not easy when you were dangling by your finger-tips four hundred metres above some *very* solid ground.

The helipad loomed beneath them like a crater on the moon. Little people scampered around gesticulating at them, as if what they had to say could possibly matter under present circumstances.

'Eddie!' cried Boudica.

Then they were slowing.

'When we're low enough,' Eddie ordered, 'let go of me and try to keep yourself loose. Try to roll with the impact. 'Fraid it's gonna hurt!'

They were at tree height. House height. Wall height. Boudica held on until her feet were trailing along the ruined helipad almost as if she was running and then she was dropping away from him and the torture in his arm was relieved and though she thudded heavily against the concrete she was going to live.

Eddie should have taken his own advice. His landing was far from textbook. Not that he cared for any kind of reading material just at the moment. Sometimes simply being alive was all that mattered.

Miraculously, Bowler was by his side. 'Gently, Master Edward,' he heard, as hands helped him ease the jet pack from his shoulders.

'Hi, Bowler. Did you miss me?' He managed a tired smile.

'Your arm, Master Edward. It appears to be in need of medical attention.'

'I guess so. If we can avoid amputation I'll be grateful. How's Rose?'

'Miss Rose is perfectly well, Master Edward, quite out of harm's way. You'll see her shortly.'

Eddie turned his gaze to the jagged wreckage of the Millennium Halls. 'Gonna be a heck of a clear-up.'

'Indeed,' said Bowler. 'At least the technicians were able to recirculate clean air before the roof and walls were breached. The Pendragon virus will not be spreading over half of London.'

'So we can all breathe easy.'

'Smiling through your pain, Master Edward. Most commendable. And it seems Mr Knight's plane has been apprehended and its occupants, most of whom were for some reason unconscious, taken into custody.'

'Excellent, Bowler. Then it's been a good day in the end for everyone but . . . where *is* Boudica?'

She was being assisted towards him by two members of the security staff, her body scuffed and bruised. Tears were streaming down her cheeks.

'Boudica,' ventured Eddie, 'why are you crying?'

'Don't you know?' She gazed at him brokenly. 'My father's dead.'

IGC DATA-FILE 2066

SUB-SECTION: GREAT BRITAIN MEDIA FEED

The Prime Minister, Peregrine Barnes, today announced that, under emergency legislation introduced following the Albion attack on the Treaty of Europa Conference, he had authorised an Act of Incorporation to be drawn up and had indeed already signed it. 'The recent outrage only proved what I have always maintained,' the Prime Minister said, 'that the only way we can tackle and defeat the terrorist threat, finally and for ever, is for nations to come together and to stand together as one, united in determination to see peace and freedom and democracy prevail. This is why I have acted on behalf of every right-minded and reasonable citizen in the United Kingdom by proceeding with an Act of Incorporation. I know it is the right, indeed the *only* thing to do.' Great Britain now belongs to Europa.

In other news, there were a number of protests at the site of the late Bartholomew Knight's Little England estate today. The property and other assets of the former Albion leader and founder of the UK First Party were appropriated by the state following his posthumous conviction for offences under the Terrorism Act. Small groups of people, mainly elderly, chanted nationalist slogans and waved UK First banners as the motley gathering of old monuments and buildings that had been collected on the estate were demolished in order to make way for a new housing development. One protestor branded the demolition as 'an act of cultural vandalism unprecedented in the history of our nation', but the prevailing view was perhaps most succinctly summarised by one of the workmen: 'The old making way for the new. That's life, innit?'

There were congratulations from Jonathan Deveraux himself which Eddie accepted with appropriate modesty and a string of self-effacing comments all pretty much along the lines of 'I only did what any graduate of Spy High would have done.'

Eddie Nelligan, Edward Red, secret agent and all-round good guy, had finally made the grade.

Considerately, Deveraux had arranged a new base of operations for him, the Camden Town location no longer being feasible. This time it was in Ealing, on the western margins of London. It was a similar small block of apartments, only this time Eddie was the only human resident in the entire building; his neighbours, who did occasionally appear at windows and play their music and receive mail, were holograms.

'And you'll still be my liaison man, I hope?' Eddie asked, as Bowler conducted a preliminary tour of the property for Eddie and Rose.

'Apparently so, Master Edward,' Bowler said, betraying neither disappointment nor delight. 'It seems Mr Deveraux considers us to have developed an effective working relationship that he wishes to see continued.'

'I'm glad.' Eddie would have liked to have shaken Bowler firmly by the hand, but he suspected the older man would have found the gesture too demonstrative.

'Glad, Master Edward?' The eyebrows. Up they inched.

'You'd have got off too lightly otherwise.' Eddie grinned. 'I've still got to get my revenge on you in the holo-gym, Bowler.'

'Ah, Master Edward' and was that really a smile there, a twinkle in the eye, almost fatherly? – 'if you anticipate us remaining together until you have bested me in the holo-gym, one feels obliged to point out that one is due to retire in ten years' time.'

Rose laughed. Eddie gaped. 'That's not a joke, is it? Is that a joke, Bowler?'

'If you'll excuse me, Master Edward, Miss Rose.' Bowler bowed and removed himself from the room, a butler returning to his household duties.

'Well, at least he's as tactful as ever,' Eddie observed. 'He knows we want to be alone.'

'Do we?' said Rose coyly.

'Don't we?' He held out his arms for her.

'Are you sure they're strong enough, particularly *that* one?'

'Good as new.'

Rose smiled. 'In that case . . .' She allowed herself to be enfolded, snuggled up to Eddie. Her expression gradually became more thoughtful. 'Eddie, what's going to happen to Boudica now?'

Eddie sighed. Why was it still impossible for him simply to categorise Boudica Knight as a Bad Guy like her father and Frankie Garvey and all the others he'd faced? Why did it still matter to him what happened to her? 'Oh, she'll go through the system,' he supposed. 'The same as Garvey and the rest. There'll be a trial. She'll be found guilty. I mean, she is guilty. She'll end up serving twenty-five to thirty in prison. That's a long time to spend pondering the error of your ways.'

'With a different father,' Rose reflected, 'perhaps Boudica would have been different.'

'Maybe.'

'I know I've got a lot to learn about the surface world yet, Eddie, but I wonder, what creates evil men like Bartholomew Knight? What makes them mad?'

'It can be a crazy world, Rose,' said Eddie. 'There's darkness in it, and greed, and murder, and all sorts of bad. That's why the Deveraux organisation's needed, why Spy High was founded, why I'm Edward Red. It's our job to guard against what's evil and to fight it wherever it's to be found. Because there's plenty of good in the world too, Rose, it's full of wonders and beauty and amazing things. And they're all out there, they're all out there just waiting for you.'

'Show me,' said Rose.

About the Author

AJ Butcher has been aware of the power of words since avoiding a playground beating aged seven because he 'told good stories'. He's been trying to do the same thing ever since. Writing serial stories at school that went on forever gave him a start (if not a finish). A degree in English Literature at Reading University kept him close to books, while a subsequent career as an advertising copywriter was intended to keep him creative. As it seemed to be doing a better job of keeping him inebriated, he finally became an English teacher instead. His influences include Dickens and Orwell, though Stan Lee, creator of the great Marvel super-heroes, is also an inspirational figure. In his spare time, AJ reads too many comics, listens to too many 70s records and rants about politics to anyone who'll listen. When he was younger and fantasising about being a published author, he always imagined he'd invent a dashing, dynamic pseudonym for himself. Now that it's happened, however, he's sadly proven too vain for that. AJ. Butcher is his real and only name.